"There're some markin[...] [...] know it happened afte[r she was dead. She was probably] wearing a necklace of some sort and the thief took it after she died."

"Could they be ligature marks? Was she strangled?" Sharyn asked.

"I don't think so. They aren't really deep enough for the force it would take to strangle her. And no bruising. I think it was an afterthought. It was probably jerked from her throat."

"So you think she was killed and then robbed?"

"Probably." Nick shrugged. "I'll know more when I do the autopsy. She's been dead for a while. Maybe twenty-four hours or more. Look at her eyes, Sharyn."

Sharyn looked at the woman more closely. "Ruptured blood vessels."

"She may have been suffocated," Nick surmised. "Possibly with that extra pillow."

"Did you get pictures?" she asked Ed.

He nodded. "Joe took some. It's almost like she knew she was going to be robbed."

"Why?" Sharyn looked at him.

"Why else wouldn't she give her real name? Maybe she was trying to protect herself."

"Probably for the same reason most people who stay here don't give their real names. Everyone here has something to hide."

★

Previously published Worldwide Mystery titles by
JOYCE & JIM LAVENE

ONE LAST GOOD-BYE
LAST DANCE
THE LAST TO REMEMBER
UNTIL OUR LAST EMBRACE
FOR THE LAST TIME

Dreams Don't Last

Joyce & Jim Lavene

TORONTO • NEW YORK • LONDON
AMSTERDAM • PARIS • SYDNEY • HAMBURG
STOCKHOLM • ATHENS • TOKYO • MILAN
MADRID • WARSAW • BUDAPEST • AUCKLAND

Recycling programs
for this product may
not exist in your area.

DREAMS DON'T LAST

A Worldwide Mystery/May 2013

First published by Avalon Books.

ISBN-13: 978-0-373-26848-1

Copyright © 2002 by Joyce & Jim Lavene

Printed in U.S.A.

Dedicated to the people of Badin, North Carolina,
the *real* home of Sheriff Sharyn Howard!
Thanks for graciously sharing the Uwharrie Mountains and
Narrows Reservoir with us!

PROLOGUE

As Senator Caison Talbot stepped out of his car he was immediately soaked to the skin. The wind and rain were sweeping down from the Uwharrie Mountains, slicing the leaves from the summer trees. Even though it was supposed to be near ninety degrees that day, the icy rain brought a chill to the early morning air.

Lightning flashed, illuminating the senator's thatch of white hair, his taut face. He fumbled with the keys to the old mill that loomed over him, finally finding the right one. He quickly opened the door and stepped inside.

There was no power. It had gone off all over the area surrounding Talbot's Mill. The small flashlight he held was like a firefly in the total black. Rats scurried along the old stone corridors on the two floors above him. There were always rats around the corn and grain. He *knew* that sound; it was one of his earliest recollections.

It was the other sound that bothered him. Footsteps were purposely scraping across the gritty floor. He looked up, and a bright light flashed in his face. He lifted a hand to shield his eyes. Thunder rolled loudly through the valley, over the lake behind the mill. It shook the old wooden beams around him. Lightning cracked, louder than the sound of gunfire, and the senator sank to his knees.

ONE

"Nurse! Nurse!" a voice called frantically from the tent. "I need more bandages!"

Sheriff Sharyn Howard sighed and went for more gauze. The long dress she wore, complete with starched crinoline and wide hoop skirt, made it impossible to move quickly over the wet lawn.

It was almost one hundred degrees that afternoon, and humid as a sauna. No breeze ruffled the treetops. She wasn't sure how the women of the Old South had managed, much less borne children and worked the fields, dressed in all these clothes. She kept promising herself a swim in the lake when it was all over. In the meantime, she smiled for the cameras.

Election fever had gripped the county. Once she'd declared her bid for reelection, her opponent, Roy Tarnower, had moved quickly to secure the lead in the polls. This had worried her party so much that they'd assigned an image consultant to help her out.

And that led to her present predicament. She'd wanted to go to the old mill festival and Revolutionary War reenactment as the sheriff, in clothes appropriate to the 1700's, of course. Her *handler* insisted that the people of Diamond Springs and Montgomery County wanted to see her as a woman. He felt that she wasn't feminine enough to inspire the female voters, and that she threatened the male voters with her power.

Sharyn went along with it because she was willing to do what the party thought was best. She wanted to win reelection and she could only blame herself that some of the voters were having a hard time making up their minds—she hadn't declared her intention to run until it was almost too late. Roy had been stumping for months with District Attorney Jack Winter at his side. Together, they were a powerful force. She was stuck playing catch-up.

Sharyn Howard was the first woman elected sheriff in the state of North Carolina. She'd been sheriff for almost one full term since her father, T. Raymond, had been killed in a convenience store robbery. She know that no one could measure the full effect of voter sympathy that might have thrust her into public office in the first election. But four years later, everything was different: she was standing on her own record.

"Where do we put the dead guys?" two of the field-corps men asked, carrying a stretcher with a man on it.

"Anywhere you can find room." She removed a huge roll of gauze from the supply kit.

The two men put down the stretcher. Sharyn looked at the boots sticking out of the dirty sheet on the crude carrier. She *knew* those boots. "I see you found the easy way out of this."

"I volunteered to come," the deep voice replied. Its owner didn't move the sheet from his face. "I didn't volunteer to charge up and down that hill all day."

"So you thought you'd become a casualty?"

"I have a good working relationship with dead people."

Sharyn shook her head. "I thought you liked playing with guns."

Nick Thomopolis, the Montgomery County medical examiner, peeked out at her from under one end of the sheet. "You're just mad because they made you wear that tablecloth getup."

"You would be, too, if you were wearing three petticoats and all this other stuff. Why did women wear so much underwear back then?"

"It was to preserve their purity," sheriff's deputy Ed Robinson told her, coming around the corner of the supply shack. He was filthy. Red dirt and black powder stains covered his clothes and hands. He wiped a careless hand across his face. "You're lucky. Being a soldier is no fun."

"I told her that," Nick replied calmly. He covered his face again, crossed his hands on his chest, and lay back on the stretcher.

"Nurse!" the doctor called again.

"Coming!" She glanced at Ed. "Playing nurse to David's doctor isn't any fun either. I'm thinking about filing a lawsuit against him for harassment and abuse!"

Ed and Nick both laughed as Sharyn went back to the tent where *Doctor* David Matthews was performing his field surgery. Mostly, this consisted of pretending to saw body parts off of a mannequin to the constant amazement of the visitors to the festival who lined up to watch him.

"Thank goodness you're back with the gauze," Doctor David declared for the benefit of the audience. He winked at a pretty girl in white shorts and a green halter-top.

Deputy David Matthews was recovering from another broken heart. His last girlfriend, new deputy Cari Long, was dating someone else. He was having a quick recovery, despite the fact that Cari's new boyfriend was his uncle, Ed Robinson.

"Now, some of the best surgeons in the field could sever a leg or an arm in only a few seconds." He ran through his speech for the watchful crowd. "Their patients had nothing for pain, and many didn't recover from the trauma."

He sawed off the mannequin's arm. People gasped at the effect. David flirted with the girl again while her parents scowled at their young son, who wanted to look at the severed arm more closely to see if there was blood.

"Are you really a doctor?" the pretty blond wondered, wide-eyed.

"No," he responded proudly. "I'm a sheriff's deputy."

"Oh." She curled her hair around her finger, smacked her gum, and looked away.

"But I'm trained to deliver babies and perform CPR."

"Oh!" The girl smiled and tossed back her mane of blond hair. "That must be exciting!"

Sharyn looked away, trying not to grimace. David had his own charm, she supposed. They'd graduated from Diamond Springs High School together. She recalled that he'd been popular in school. He'd joined the sheriff's office before her father was killed. He didn't hide the fact that he still resented that she had been elected sheriff with no experience in the field.

"Sheriff?"

Sharyn turned around and smiled at Ernie Watkins, her head deputy.

"She's my *nurse* in this tent," David corrected him.

"Is she the sheriff?" the blond girl asked him curiously. "A woman sheriff?"

"Let's go outside then, *Nurse,*" Ernie corrected. "I'd like to have a word with the sheriff."

"Wipe my fevered brow first, Nurse," Doctor David demanded.

"Old son, you'd better remember that you have to go back to work sometime, and she's still the boss," Ernie reminded him, seeing the look on Sharyn's face.

Sharyn smiled for the crowd. She wiped David's forehead with a little more force than was necessary before she followed Ernie out of the tent. "What's up?"

"I know you're gonna love this one," Ernie told her grimly. "The senator appears to be missing."

Sharyn shook her head. Her short, copper-colored curls were bright in the hot sunshine. "Missing? Caison?"

"Yep. Your mother called on the way from his place. His car is gone. He was supposed to pick her up, but he never came. She's been trying his cell phone but no response."

"What about that gopher that follows him around all the time?"

Ernie nodded. "Sloane Phillips. I gave him a call. He sounds pretty frantic. Seems he hasn't seen the senator since yesterday evening. He was supposed to come to the festival with him, too."

Sharyn stared at the shiny medals on Ernie's gray uniform. "I suppose we wouldn't be lucky enough that he ran away to another country with a fortune in taxpayer money?"

As Ernie grinned, the effect almost wiggled his ears. "Nope. I'm afraid *you* wouldn't be that lucky, Sheriff. What do you want to do?"

"My mother's on her way here?"

"You got it."

She sighed. "Then I guess we look for Senator Talbot. Call Joe at the office. Have him put out an APB on his car. He hasn't been missing a full twenty-four hours yet, so we can't do missing-persons on him."

"What's going on?" Ed asked, walking up to them with his arm around Cari Long. He was a good twenty years older than the girl but Ed had a way with women and he didn't look his age. His bright blue eyes and curly blond hair complimented his dimples and his long, lean body.

"Senator Talbot's missing," Sharyn explained.

"And we're planning the party?"

"Ed!" Ernie warned.

"Okay. Seriously. Do we *want* to find him?"

"Want to find who?" Nick asked from his spot in the shade of an enormous hickory tree.

"Caison Talbot is missing," Ed supplied. "Nothing for you to do, *yet*."

"Ed!" Sharyn cautioned.

"Well, it's true! Not one of us would shed a tear if that man was never found," Ed argued. "And some of us, *Sheriff,* would breathe easier because he wasn't about to be our new daddy!"

Sharyn ignored him. "Get that APB going, Ernie. After Joe sets it up, have him take a drive over to the senator's place. Have him meet the senator's aid there."

"Sheriff?" Her PR man called out. "I've been looking for you everywhere!"

She frowned as Don James came huffing up the big hill from the lakeside. "Great. Time to play Barbie."

"Is that what you call it?" Nick asked.

Ernie glanced at the body beneath the sheet. "Nick, for a medical examiner, you're way too comfortable on that stretcher."

"Will it make you feel better if I promise not to do my own autopsy?"

"It'd make me feel better not to *have* an autopsy," Ed said, hugging Cari. "I want to die in my bed surrounded by my twelve kids and sixty grandchildren."

Ernie laughed as he took out his cell phone. "You gotta get started first! And the way you're going, you won't have time for that many kids!"

Ed smiled into Cari's pretty face. "You never know, Ernie."

Cari stroked her hand through his short blond curly hair and smiled into his big blue eyes.

"What's going on out here?" Doctor David demanded, coming out of the tent. He glared at Ed and Cari. "I need my nurse."

"You'll have to get by," Ernie told him. "They want to take pictures of her down by the lake."

David glared at his uncle and his ex-girlfriend again and then went back into the tent.

"Let's get going," Sharyn added, glancing at her arm. She'd left her digital wristwatch behind. None of the reenactors were allowed to wear anything that hadn't been available during the Revolutionary War. "Does anyone know what time it is?"

"According to my calculations," Ed said, calculating the angle of the sun, "it's close to 3:00 p.m."

"That's pretty good," Nick said. "It's three fifteen." "You weren't supposed to wear that watch!" Sharyn reminded him.

Nick shrugged and pulled the dark blue uniform sleeve over the timepiece. "What are they going to do, shoot me?"

"It's an interesting idea at times," Sharyn remarked, picking up the edge of her skirt.

"He's got you outgunned, Sheriff," Ed told her lazily. "Joe's taking care of the APB," Ernie told Sharyn. "Sure you don't want to help him?"

Sharyn was tempted. "No, I promised the party I'd try to work with Don. And the senator could be coming late for effect. Who knows?"

"Sheriff." The tall, thin PR man reached her at last.

He tried to catch his breath. "We're waiting for you. Are you ready? You look fabulous!"

"I want to watch," Cari said with a smile at Ed. The faint breeze ruffled her long, straight blond hair and her brown eyes looked longingly at him.

"Let's go!" Ed agreed.

The old Talbot Mill had been standing for two hundred and fifty years. It had been in the hands of the Montgomery County historical society for the past fifty years. Once a year, they held the summer festival and reenactment of the battle that took place on the grounds around the mill.

Senator Caison Talbot's great-grandfather had built the mill from native rock and put the first grist stone in place. He'd been, by all accounts, a cantankerous man who'd lived to be a hundred years old and sired a line of Talbots that stretched across the county. His son had been a district court judge. The current senator's father had been a governor. Talbot money and influence went back further than anyone could recall. Senator Talbot was running unopposed in the district in the present election. He would, doubtless, see another term in office.

More importantly to Sharyn, Caison Talbot was going to marry her mother after the election. He'd been a good friend of her father's and started dating her mother when Faye Howard had asked him for help two years before. Sharyn had been about to investigate a murder case that T. Raymond, her father, had closed. Caison had tried to persuade her to leave it alone.

But Sharyn not only looked like her father and the Howard clan, she was as stubborn as any of them. She'd found out that her father had been wrong about the man he'd arrested for committing the murder. That made Caison, as prosecuting attorney on that case, wrong too. But it was like a raindrop in a storm compared to the man's popularity in the district. Sharyn couldn't imagine anything that would prevent the senator from being elected again.

"You look wonderful," Don confided, standing close to Sharyn. "Your cheeks are rosy, your hair looks—does anyone have a mobcap to keep her hair from catching fire in the sun?"

"Yeah," Ed declared with a grin. "Might burn a hole in those TV cameras!"

"Like a laser," Nick added.

"I have a scarf," Cari volunteered, drawing it from her pocket.

"Did they have scarves in the 1700s?" Nick asked quietly, studying Sharyn's face as they fluttered around her. She had a high boiling point but when she reached it, there was no going back.

"I'm not sure," Don confided, his hand spiking up his already spiky blond hair.

"I have a shawl, too," Cari offered.

"I'm not wearing a shawl on my head," Sharyn finally told them. "Or a scarf. I have red hair. If people don't want to vote for me because of it, then I won't be the sheriff again!"

"That's right," her aunt, Selma Howard said, coming to her side. "And there's nothing wrong with red hair!"

Don James looked at the elder Howard's full head of curly red hair streaked with white and relented. "You'll be fine. The senator was supposed to dedicate the wildlife preserve with you at his side. Then you were supposed to say a few words about ecology in Montgomery County. I'm not sure what we're doing now. Does anyone know where Senator Talbot is?"

The mock Revolutionary War battle was coming closer to where they were standing on a path overlooking the lake. The loud retorts of the cannons and the exploding gunshots echoed around them.

"Do they go all the way down to the lake?" Don asked, finding the noise distracting.

"They charge down the hill but the fighting stops before they reach the water," Selma told him. "They didn't fire on the mill. I suppose they figured even a patriot had to eat!"

Selma walked with Sharyn towards the podium set up beside the river for the event. "You look irritated."

Sharyn rolled her eyes at her aunt. "This election might be more work than it's worth."

"How much is that, Sharyn?"

"I'm not sure yet," her niece replied. "I'll let you know if I get there."

"I checked in with JP and Joe at the office," Ernie said to Sharyn. "Joe just left to go to the senator's place. JP is holding down the fort at the office. Everything's been quiet."

"Good," Sharyn replied. "If we get swamped, we'll send Nick since he's already dead here."

"But he's the M.E.," Cari reminded her with a confused look at Ed.

"He's also a fully deputized officer of the law," Ed told her.

"Yeah," Sharyn said. "And he has the guns to prove it!"

"Can we lay off the wisecracks about my guns?" Nick questioned.

The trees shook with the roar of the cannons from the hill. At least two hundred men and women were taking part in the event that weekend, coming from as far away as California and Idaho. They were all dedicated to preserving the past with their demonstrations and their attention to detail. Many of them had been coming to Talbot's Mill to fight the old battle for twenty years.

"Those cannons sound real, don't they?" Cari asked Ed, moving a little closer to him.

"They are real," Nick told her. "The charges are real, anyway. They're just not loaded."

"Isn't that dangerous?" Don James asked nervously as he watched the battle flow down the hill towards them.

"Relax," Ed explained. "They're firing blanks."

"All they can do is deafen you," Selma added.

Cari looked across at the green grassy hill. "I'm surprised some of the men aren't seriously hurt. They really make a good show of it."

"Some of them are," Ed said. "I broke my wrist out here two years ago when a friend of mine charged me."

Sharyn saw Roy Tarnower and a few of the county commissioners setting up for their turns at the microphone. Roy had been sheriff of Diamond Springs for one term between her grandfather, Jacob, and her father. He'd filed a lawsuit protesting her running for sheriff when her father was killed, but nothing had ever come of it. He was a heavyset man with a bulldog's face and a thick head of black hair that didn't show a speck of gray, even though she knew he had to be close to sixty.

Roy was backed by Jack Winter because he represented "business as usual" in Diamond Springs. That included the D.A. and some of the older power brokers who pulled the strings. She wasn't sure why Caison was backing her for sheriff, since he and Winter were longtime friends and partners in crime. She could only imagine all the things they were guilty of doing together in the past. Her father may have been involved in some shady things when he was sheriff. Winter had hinted at it often enough.

All she was sure of was that she was dedicated to bringing the D.A. down. He'd offered her a job working at his side if she'd give up being sheriff. She'd finished law school; she'd just never gone back to take the Bar exam. She'd considered it before she'd decided to run for sheriff again—to go back to the life she'd planned before her father had died.

But it wasn't right for her anymore. She knew that now. Diamond Springs was changing as more and more people moved there from all across the country. Charlotte, the closest large city to the west, was spilling across its borders and into Diamond Springs. It was time to run things differently.

That meant no more dark rooms and secrets that only a few powerful men kept hidden. That was why she'd decided to run again: because she felt she could make a difference.

"Sheriff," Roy Tarnower acknowledged her.

"Mr. Tarnower."

The old water wheel turned slowly behind them as water from the lake was released slowly from the dam. Sharyn learned as a child that the corn was pulverized inside the mill by two giant stones attached to the wheel. The little mill still produced grits and cornmeal for the tourists.

"You're looking very…appropriate," Tarnower said, assessing her from the edge of her skirt to the top of her head.

It was one of the few times Sharyn wished she was wearing her uniform and carrying her grandfather's WWII service revolver. The tan-and-brown uniform was designed for a man and made her slightly square body and face look worse. But at least she *felt* like the sheriff. She looked down at her dress and decided that it would have to do; she *was* the sheriff of Diamond Springs. She didn't need a uniform and a gun to have authority. Her father had taught her that.

"Thank you, sir," she answered calmly. "It's a wonderful day for the festival, isn't it?"

Foster Odom, star reporter for the Diamond Springs *Gazette,* shook his graying blond hair at their remarks. "Is *this* what we have to look forward to today? Where's the fire and the rhetoric?"

"The fire is there behind us," Sharyn reminded him as the battle continued to grow noisier with each passing moment. "As for the rhetoric—"

Roy Tarnower hitched up his belt and walked away towards the TV news crew.

"I see the party thought you needed a keeper," Foster said to Sharyn, nodding his head at Don James.

"Please," Don admonished. "I'm her *consultant.*"

JOYCE & JIM LAVENE

"What are you consulting with her about?"

Don smiled quickly but it didn't reach his eyes. "The sheriff and I are working on her campaign strategy and I—"

The last volley of musket fire exploded close by. Smoke made the air around the mill hazy. It smelled of sulphur and black powder. It was easy to imagine the real battle that had taken place there.

A woman screamed but it was impossible to tell where it came from.

"Is that part of the reenactment?" Cari asked.

"I don't think so," Sharyn said. "I think it came from the mill." She lifted the edges of her skirt and began to run down the gravel path towards the old mill.

Ernie was on his cell phone right behind her. Nick, Cari, and Ed were following quickly when they heard the woman scream again.

A group of visitors came running out of the mill. "There was blood!"

"I saw a man sliding out of the corn chute," a woman related loudly. "He was covered in blood and cornmeal!"

"Where?" Sharyn asked, coming up close to them. "Near the grinding stone," the woman told her. "It was terrible!"

Sharyn pushed past the next group running from

the mill. She ran to the second floor and looked down the chute.

"Sheriff! Down here!" the mill operator called. Gathering up her skirt, she slid down the chute through the leftover cornmeal and got to her feet at the bottom. A man was lying on the stone floor, covered in blood and cornmeal as the visitors had told her. She couldn't tell if he was dead or alive as she pushed aside the meal that clung to him and tried to find a pulse.

"I think it's Senator Talbot," the mill operator said slowly.

Sharyn looked up at his face. "I don't know—"

"Where am I?" the prone figure asked, trying to get up. "What's going on?"

It *was* Caison Talbot.

"Nick!" Sharyn called out to the man behind her. She pushed aside her wide skirt to kneel at the senator's side in the yellow corn dust. "Take it easy, Senator. Lie back."

Nick was at her side, along with Ernie who was already calling for help. There were paramedics stationed at the perimeter of the festival in case of emergencies with the crowd.

"He's been shot," Nick said, lifting the gray sleeve from the wound.

"Shot?" Ernie demanded. "Ed, see what you can

do about getting some kind of containment around the mill! Take Cari and get David."

"This happened recently," Nick told him. "The sound of the cannons might have masked the gunshot."

Ernie looked up into the high rafters above the corn chute. "What was he doing up there?"

"I think it might be a musket ball." Nick tried to get a better look at the wound. "It nicked the artery in his shoulder. He's lost a lot of blood already."

"I can't die yet," Caison told them bluntly.

"I don't think that's going to happen, Senator," Nick replied with quiet authority.

Sharyn supported Talbot's head on her lap while Nick got the sleeve out of the way.

"The bleeding isn't as bad as it could be," Nick said, looking at the wound. "The cornmeal is probably acting as a coagulant. Nasty wound where it went in, though. It's going to be bad getting it back out."

"I can tell you usually work with dead people," Sharyn remarked caustically. She glanced at Caison's face as she wiped away the cornmeal. It was as white as his famous thatch of white hair. "It's going to be all right, Senator."

Caison glanced at Sharyn. "I do love your mother."

"I know. That's fine," she said awkwardly. "Try not to talk."

They heard the siren as the medical unit came

over the hill, almost hitting several reenactors who didn't realize what had happened. The two paramedics rushed forward and took over, admonishing Nick that he might have done more harm than good.

"I think I can handle it, junior," Nick told the first young man.

"Oh, sorry, Dr. Thomopolis! I didn't recognize you."

"I think he was hit by musket fire," Nick explained to him.

"A musket ball? Aren't they supposed to be shooting blanks?"

"Yeah, *supposed* to be."

"The guns have been stored here since Friday night. I signed the permit for it." Sharyn got to her feet as the second paramedic took her place with the senator. "There were some musket balls, too."

She was aware of the TV crew filming everything as it happened, It made the whole thing seem even more unreal. Lots of accidents happened out here every year: heat stroke, sprains, even a few broken limbs from the skirmishing. But she didn't think anyone had ever been shot.

She looked down at Caison, who had drifted into unconsciousness. Blood had seeped down his arm and across his chest. He looked helpless, and for once, at the mercy of something larger than himself. The man had enemies, there was no doubting that fact.

He'd probably made enemies even *he* wasn't aware of with his blustering and his power plays.

"Only one of the guns fired that ball," Nick replied. "There must be a way to tell which one."

She nodded. "And only two or three hundred to go through to find out."

"What was he doing up there alone?" Ernie wondered as the paramedics lifted the senator onto the stretcher. "The man doesn't go to the bathroom without an escort!"

Sharyn grimaced. "We've probably lost any forensics that might have been here."

"I'll call Keith and get a team out here," Nick said, taking out his cell phone.

"Let's see if we can find the senator's car," Sharyn suggested. "If he was here alone, he must have driven himself. Ernie, get Joe on the line and find out if Mr. Phillips had any idea of the senator's intentions. He had to be out here for some reason."

"Yes, ma'am."

"Sharyn, Faye's here. I'm going to take her to the hospital," Selma told her. "If there's word about anything, we'll be there."

"Thanks, Aunt Selma," Sharyn said. She glimpsed her mother's tear-stained face in the crowd at the door.

"So, what's next?" Nick asked gruffly, seeing the look on her face.

Sharyn forced herself to look away from her mother's expression. "First, we round up all the weapons that were stored here and tag them for evidence. Then we sit down and talk to the reenactors, and find out if any of them are bad shots. Who else would shoot a man with a musket?"

Ernie shrugged. "Maybe whoever it was didn't come here to kill the senator, but something got out of control."

"That line would probably go out the door and around the corner," Nick said coolly. "Starting with Ed and Sharyn."

Sharyn nodded. "I know. Do you know anyone who knows about forensics on muskets?"

TWO

IT WAS DUSK before they had gathered together all the muskets and firearms that the reenactors were carrying. There were a few illegal guns being carried without permits. The reenactors complained loudly about the sheriff's department harassing them, but the Montgomery County Historical Society complained even louder.

"We rely on reenactors coming from across the country to this festival, Sheriff," Anjelica Parsons from the historical society told her. "If they start getting panicked and put out the word that it's a bad place to come—"

"I appreciate your concern, Ms. Parsons," Sharyn sympathized with her. "But someone shot the senator, and we have to find out how that happened."

"You don't think one of the reenactors did it, do you?" Anjelica demanded. "Anyone could have broken into the mill and had access to those guns. There were hundreds of people here."

"I know, ma'am. But firing a musket takes specialized knowledge that most of the visitors probably don't have. The reenactors have that knowledge.

I have to go through all the steps. I'm sure you can understand why."

"I can." Anjelica cooled herself with a painted fan. "I just hope it will be finished soon, Sheriff."

"Just got the word from the hospital," Ernie told her, coming up from behind the departing woman. "Senator Talbot's gonna be fine. And it *was* a musket ball in his shoulder. Nick was right."

"I do know a few things about entry wounds," Nick said. "We've got all the muskets tagged. I put in a call to a friend of mine in Raleigh. He's the only person I know in this state who can tell us which of these muskets fired the ball."

"Why's that so hard?" Sharyn asked.

"Because with the powder charge in them for show, all of the muskets will look as though they've been fired," Nick explained. "Only an expert on antique firearms will know the difference. Since the senator could have died, I thought you'd want to be sure."

Sharyn nodded in agreement as she looked at the list of reenactors. There were almost three hundred on the list. All of them were being detained in their cars, trucks and vans until she gave the word to let them go. "Did any of you pick up on anything unusual when you were talking with them?"

Ernie shook his head. "Everyone I talked to was from out of state. I got the feeling none of them knows Talbot."

"Same here," David replied. "There were a few locals but I know them all. I don't think any of them has a grudge against Senator Talbot. And I think if they did, they'd use something besides a musket and they would've killed him."

"That's a good point," Ed added. "I think if it was planned, Senator Talbot would be dead from a real bullet—not some old iron ball."

"Those musket balls can cause more damage than a real bullet," Nick told them. "I've only read about them historically but they were pretty bad."

"But the muskets themselves are hard to aim and harder to use. The barrels are crooked. If someone came here to kill Talbot, he wouldn't use a musket," Ed asserted.

"Maybe they just meant to scare him," Cari said with a shrug, almost lost in the interplay between the group who'd worked so closely together. It was always hard to find a spot to jump into the conversation.

Sharyn nodded. "We have all their names and addresses from reliable sources, right?"

They all agreed.

"Okay. Nick, if you'd send those muskets to your friend, I'd appreciate it."

"The commission isn't going to want to foot that bill!" Ernie said with a whistle.

"No, they won't. But the press from this should convince them it's necessary," Sharyn decided. "Let's process the illegal firearms and the people who had them. Tell the rest of them they're free to go."

IT ONLY TOOK the county commission a few hours to scare up some press and three commissioners the next morning. By 10:00 a.m., Sharyn was in the hot seat.

"And can you explain again *why* you felt it was necessary to take two hundred muskets from their owners and ship them across the state?" Ty Swindoll asked her.

The commissioners were supposed to be investigating all of the events of the previous day, but everything had come down to why Sharyn had chosen to spend a large amount of money on shipping the guns. There was also the issue, as presented by Anjelica Parsons, about the reenactors being made to feel as though they were criminals.

"Mr. Swindoll," Sharyn began, addressing the commissioner who'd always been her most vocal opponent, "Senator Talbot was shot by a musket."

"During a *mock* battle, Sheriff," Commissioner Betty Fontana added her voice. "I'm sure we have to allow for some hazards in that situation? Couldn't it have been an accident?"

"No, ma'am. The muskets weren't supposed to be loaded. I think we have to assume that if someone loaded one and pointed it at the senator, he or she meant business. We haven't been able to talk with the senator yet but the law requires that the sheriff's office investigate *any* shooting. That's all we were doing at the mill yesterday. Questioning the reenactors was unfortunate, but we needed to have their names and addresses to match to their guns. One of them was loaded, ma'am. And it could have cost the senator his life."

"Sheriff, in these cost-conscious times," Reed Harker, the head commissioner, addressed her, "wasn't there a better way to have the muskets examined?"

"Sir, Dr. Thomopolis only knew of one expert in the state who was qualified to tell if the musket had been fired. A musket is an antique firearm, not all gun experts are qualified. Our gun expert, Harold Swinson, has never handled a musket. He doesn't know what to look for."

"Still, Sheriff," Ty Swindoll surged forward for the benefit of the press who were watching the event, "it's going to cost the county almost six hundred dollars to send those guns to Raleigh! Was that the best you could do?"

Ernie and Joe stirred, restless and impatient behind her as the press and the commissioners waited for her response to the question. Everyone knew Ty Swindoll had given the sheriff a hard time since he'd taken over from George Albert, the previous commissioner. Swindoll was from the new, expensive suburbs growing just outside of Diamond Springs.

Sharyn stared at him. A hundred retorts came to mind. Each of them was strangled before it reached her lips. Finally, she spoke. Her voice rang confidently through the room. "Commissioner Swindoll, I understand that you have a minivan. The guns won't leave for another hour. Can you offer the county a competitive price to take the guns to Raleigh?"

All eyes shifted to Swindoll, where he sat on the dais beside the other two commissioners hastily thrown together for a meeting.

Reed Harker cleared his throat. Betty Fontana touched up her lipstick. They both avoided looking at their contemporary. It was every commissioner for him or herself in the election year.

"I have a business to run, Sheriff," Swindoll told her shortly. "Much as I'd like to be able to save the taxpayers this money, I don't have the time. If this is the best price you could get for transport, I guess it will have to do."

"Thank you, sir," Sharyn replied, taking a deep breath.

The meeting finished with the commissioners telling Sharyn to keep them posted on the events surrounding the shooting. The press put away their cameras and tape recorders as the room emptied out.

"This place twists my stomach up in a knot," Ernie whispered as they started out the door.

"I'd like to take that Swindoll and wring his neck," Joe confessed in a low growl.

"Oh, Sheriff?" Commissioner Swindoll called as she was leaving.

"Commissioner?" She nodded to him as she waited for him to catch up with her. Ernie and Joe flanked her as though they were ready to shoot it out at her back. Joe put on his mirrored sunglasses and folded his arms against his chest.

Ty Swindoll's narrow face was sharply intelligent. He pushed at his thinning hair and shook his head. "I just wanted you to know that I'm glad you decided to run for office again. You're a good sheriff."

He nodded to Ernie and Joe then hurried out into the hot sunlight on the steps of the courthouse.

"Say *what?*" Ernie asked when he was gone.

"He's gotta have a split personality," Joe decided.

"You just can't take it personally," Sharyn reminded them. "And if there's one thing I've learned after almost four years, it's that you can't tell your enemies because they treat you like gold, and you can't tell your friends because they treat you like trash."

"That's profound," Joe remarked as they stepped out into the heat.

"Yeah. When did you get so profound?" Ernie wondered.

"Isn't there someplace we can post that?" Joe teased.

"Okay, okay!" She laughed. "See if I ever tell either of you anything again! Now that the commission meeting is over, let's get some work done."

SHARYN ALREADY HAD Cari working her way through the names and addresses of the reenactors as she logged them into the computer. She added Ernie to that assignment as well to try to get the job done faster. Joe went out on patrol with Ed.

"I'm going to the hospital to see the senator," she told Ernie. "The doctor said he's conscious. He must have heard or seen something. And I'd like to know what he was doing up there alone."

"If he doesn't know *exactly* who was behind that musket," Ernie replied quietly.

"How likely would he be to tell anyone even if he does know?"

"Not too likely. He'd probably want to take care of it personally."

"Which could mean another homicide."

Ernie laughed as his fingers flew across the keyboard. "The senator would never be that indiscreet, Sheriff!"

Sharyn shrugged and put on her hat. "I'm going to have to talk to him anyway. Even if he doesn't want to tell me anything."

"Good luck."

"Thanks." She walked up to Trudy's desk. "I'm going to the hospital. I'll be back after lunch."

"Got it, Sheriff!"

Foster Odom almost walked into her as she was coming down the steps of the sheriff's office. "So, Sheriff, who do you think shot the good senator? Or do you think it was an accident?"

Sharyn considered her answer carefully. "We don't have enough information to make that judgment, Mr. Odom."

He smiled as he wrote her words. "Very well put, Sheriff! I guess some of that Don James fella is rubbing off on you, huh? You weren't always so diplomatic!"

"Being sheriff wasn't always such a diplomatic job, Mr. Odom."

"You still owe me that personal interview, you know," he reminded her, following her down the steps to the sidewalk.

"Make an appointment with Trudy, Mr. Odom. I'm on my way to the hospital."

"To visit the senator?"

"Yes."

"Great! I can come with you."

"In place of the interview?"

He considered it. "Nope. You won't get out of it

that easy, Sheriff! I'm going to make that appointment right now."

"*Great!* Goodbye, Mr. Odom."

"Until later, Sheriff Howard."

SHARYN WALKED QUICKLY towards the hospital. There were rain clouds gathering on the top of the mountains. They were in for some moisture, and the temperatures would cool off for a while. They needed some real rain, though, not the hard, fast thunderstorms that had swept through the past few nights.

It had been a dry summer after a short, dry winter. That combination created a threat of forest fires in the Uwharries, and the possibility of water shortages in the outlying areas around Diamond Springs. The area was growing too fast to keep pace with schools or water supplies. Still, the commission kept granting building permits.

Eventually, she knew, taxes from the most expensive houses would begin to fill the county coffers, but until then, it was going to be rough going. The sheriff's department had received an unexpected boon from the commission. She'd been able to hire Cari with it, and there was enough money left over for a new squad car and possibly another deputy.

With all of the commissioners up for reelection, she meant to hold on to some of that money. Who knew what the new commission would bring? A tiny

JOYCE & JIM LAVENE

voice inside her wondered if she would be the sheriff who would deal with them.

"Going my way?" a familiar voice caught her as she started up the steps to the redbrick hospital.

"No, actually, I'm here to visit the living for a change," she told Nick as she turned to face him. "Well, when I'm not in here for myself."

"You've had your share," he replied.

"I heard that the senator is up and driving everyone crazy. I thought I'd ask him a few questions in case he wants me to catch who did this."

"Mind if I tag along?"

"No." She glanced around them. "Don't you have something you'd rather do?"

"Trying to get rid of me?"

She looked down into his face. She'd made up her mind that she was going to feel differently about Nick. Of course, she'd done that before and it never seemed to work. The problem was that she was attracted to him but she'd never had much luck with relationships. The longest one she'd ever had lasted about two weeks. And that was before she'd been elected sheriff.

Since then, there hadn't been time for anything. Except for this man, whom she thought she hated, was coming perilously close to making an imprint on her heart. She could tell herself whatever she wanted in the moments before she went to sleep or while she was driving around, but the truth was, she cared for him.

She didn't know if he cared for her or not. For the first few years that she'd been sheriff, he'd resigned as medical examiner because of their differences, and generally given her a hard time. But in the last year or so, things had been different between them. *He'd* been different. He'd held her hand for support and listened to her ideas. He'd kissed her (or at least she *thought* he'd kissed her) the last time she'd been in the hospital after being injured on the job.

They'd never spoken of the event. She'd thought that he'd hinted at it once or twice, but apparently, if it *had* happened, neither of them were brave enough to admit it.

All of these things raced through her mind as she looked at his dark eyes and silver-streaked black hair. Nick was about eight years older than she. He'd worked with her father and Ernie before she was sheriff. He wasn't from Diamond Springs, but she'd grown to like him being there.

"No," she admitted finally. "I was just thinking that I'd want to be anywhere else except talking to Caison!"

"Really?" He looked into her eyes and knew that she was lying. He'd come to know so much about her in the last few years. Most of it was through observation. One thing he knew for sure—she was the worst liar in the world.

"No," she hedged. "Come on. Let's go and talk to Caison."

He nodded and followed her up the steps. Now, if he could just figure out what she *was* thinking about when she lied to him. *That* would be a revelation!

"How's the evidence from the old mill coming along?" she asked as they rode in the elevator together.

"I've collected about two thousand fingerprints, enough hair samples to make a coat, a few hundred footprints and some stray buttons. All I have to do is match everything to the tourists, the reenactors and the locals who were going in and out of the mill, and then decide which one shot the senator."

Sharyn arched a pale red brow at him. "And you have time for *this?*"

"That's why I have help!"

Battle-weary nurses were sitting outside the senator's room on the fourth floor. An orderly cleaning up a food tray that had been smashed against the wall told part of the story. When Sharyn saw Dr. Anderson, a doctor who'd treated her before when she'd been injured, she asked how the senator was doing.

The doctor shook her head. "I don't know what keeps him from having a heart attack right now! His blood pressure is through the roof. He's in pain and he won't take his meds—"

"What about the bullet?" Nick asked.

"Well, that was messy. We had him in surgery for four hours but we cleaned it up. No wonder so many men lost their legs and arms to those musket balls! I sent it to your office, Nick. I thought you'd probably want to see it."

"Thanks," he replied easily.

Sharyn looked at Elizabeth Anderson and Nick and considered what a great couple they would make. Both of them tall and thin, both of them doctors.

"I'm going in to see him," Sharyn said before her mind wandered any further down that path.

As she pushed open the door to the senator's room, Diamond Springs' district attorney, Jack Winter, came out. He was wearing a linen suit exactly the pale blue color of his cold eyes. When he looked at Sharyn, a chill went down her spine. She suppressed the shudder and straightened her back, not willing to give him an ounce of satisfaction at thinking she might be afraid of him.

He acknowledged her with a nod of his head and a quick glance at Nick. "Our senator makes a bad patient."

"Not surprising."

"No, not really. How are you? Things have been quiet lately. We haven't spent much time together. We should go out for dinner to get away from the shop-talk. What do you say?"

"I'd love to, sir, but my days are pretty full with the election and everything."

"Of course. Well, maybe later." He nodded to Nick. "Dr. Thomopolis."

"Mr. Winter."

Sharyn went into the room as he left. Caison was sitting in a chair near the edge of the bed. There was an IV in his arm. He looked much more frail than she'd ever seen him in his dark robe and slippers. His hair was uncombed but his vivid blue eyes were unmistakable.

"I suppose you've come to gloat?" he demanded hoarsely.

Sharyn stared at him. "Because you're hurt? Hardly."

"Then why are you here?"

"Because I'm the sheriff and a crime was committed. I need to ask you a few questions about what happened."

"Like what?"

"Like did you see anything or anyone? Do you know who shot you, Senator?"

Nick came quietly into the room beside her. Senator Talbot ignored him as he stared out the hospital window that overlooked Diamond Mountain Lake.

"I didn't hear or see anything. I knew I was hurt because I felt a pain in my arm and it felt numb. I tried to move it and found the blood. After that, I don't really remember anything until I fell down the corn chute at the mill."

"You were shot with a musket," Sharyn said.

"So they tell me."

"Do you think it could have been anyone in particular?"

He laughed, a strange sound that was like dry leaves scratching on the floor. "Young woman, it would surprise me if it wasn't *someone* in particular! I hope you're not here to ask me a bunch of mumbo jumbo about people wanting to kill me or who my enemies are because I've lost track. When you get to be my age and do the job I do, there are too many to count."

Sharyn nodded. "All right. We've sent the muskets to Raleigh to be examined by an expert. When we find which gun shot the ball at you, we can proceed from there, even if the shooter lives in another state."

He waved his hand at her. "Go away, Sharyn. I'm feeling weak."

"Just one more thing, Senator. Why were you at the mill alone? Your P.A. and my mother had already called to tell us that you were missing. You drove yourself to the mill. Why were you there?"

"Not that it's any of your business, but I was thinking about my childhood. I spent a great deal of time there when I was a child. I didn't need Sloane or your mother to go with me for that. I didn't need anyone!"

"I'm sorry to have to pry, sir," she relented. "But I'll have to keep investigating. If you can remember anything about the shooting, you should tell me."

"Go away, Sharyn. I'm tired now."

Dismissed by the senator, Sharyn and Nick walked out of the hospital room together.

"What do you think?" Nick wondered aloud as they walked to the elevator.

"I don't know," she admitted. "I really don't know. I don't think he'd tell me if he *did* know anything."

"But he might have Jack Winter murder the man for him while he's recovering in the hospital?"

The elevator doors opened and Sloane Phillips, the senator's aide, came rushing out. "Sheriff! How is he?"

"He's not saying, Mr. Phillips."

Sloane Phillips smiled slowly. He was a good-looking young man in his late twenties or early thirties with a boyish smile and a pleasant manner. He was always dressed conservatively and neatly beside the outlandish and outrageous senator.

"He's hard to get to know. He seems difficult on the outside but he's got a heart of gold."

"Mr. Phillips, has he confided in you at all about this incident?" she asked doubtfully. What were the chances the senator's aide would tell her anything if he wanted to keep his job?

"Not really. I've been with him for almost six years, but he keeps his secrets. He's a very private person. I don't know what he was doing out there alone yesterday. I know he's been moody and pensive lately. Not his usual energetic self. I'm worried that it may be his health."

"But you'd tell me if you had knowledge of anything that would help solve this crime?"

"Of course, Sheriff. The senator has been very good to me. I know the two of you don't get along. But Senator Talbot is a very complex person with great responsibilities on his shoulders."

"I understand, Mr. Phillips." Sharyn handed him her card. "If you hear anything or notice anything else unusual, please let me know."

He looked at the card then at her. "I will, Sheriff."

"Thanks."

Nick stepped into the elevator and held the door. Sharyn followed him.

"He's a good and faithful servant," he remarked.

"I didn't expect any different. He told me exactly what he told Joe."

"You just thought you could get something else out of him?"

Sharyn laughed. "I guess I thought he might succumb to my personal interviewing skills."

"You should do that more often," Nick told her.

"What?"

"Laugh. You used to be a lot happier when you were in college."

"Life changes," she answered.

"T. Raymond wouldn't want you to be miserable because of him."

"I know. And I'm not really. I miss him. I think it's this job."

"Then I was wrong," he admitted. "You shouldn't run for sheriff again."

"Nick, everyone grows up!"

"But not everyone grows unhappy because of it."

"I'm not unhappy," she argued, "just thoughtful. And you of all people shouldn't be talking about people being unhappy! What about you?"

"*I'm* not unhappy," he defended. "I'm laconic. That's different!"

The elevator doors parted and she almost jumped out of the car.

"Have lunch with me," he invited. "We haven't been spending any quality time together lately."

"It's been a while," she responded quickly, knowing the last time was the night after he'd kissed her. She knew because she'd been careful to keep it that way.

He stopped her movement towards the door with

a hand on her arm. "There's something we need to talk about."

Her cell phone started ringing and she picked it up gratefully. "Sheriff Howard."

"Sheriff, Joe and I got a call to come down to the Bridge Motel about half an hour ago. I think you should come, too—and you might want to call Nick."

"What's up, Ed?"

"We got a call about a robbery, but there's a dead woman here. Early fifties, maybe. No ID. She's still in bed in her nightgown."

Sharyn glanced at Nick. "Okay, Ed. I'll be right there."

"What's wrong?" Nick asked, seeing the look on her face.

"There might be another homicide over at the Bridge Motel."

"Why don't you close that place down and save us all some time and trouble?" he asked harshly.

"Because they'd do it somewhere else, Nick. You want to follow me over?"

"Can I hitch a ride? If I need the team, I'll call Keith from there."

She smiled weakly and nodded. Keith Reynolds was Nick's assistant. He was also her sister's ex-boyfriend. "Sure, why not. How is Keith?"

"Still pining after your sister. How is Kristie?" Nick climbed into Sharyn's Jeep.

"She won't talk. She dyed her hair purple and got her lip pierced. She isn't going to go back to school this fall and she doesn't ever want to leave the house."

"I already know how your mother and aunt are, so that concludes the small talk."

Sharyn glanced at him uneasily. "Do you always have to be this way?"

"I don't think that's fair, Sharyn. I've kept my mouth shut. I've been polite and played along like a good boy. I've watched the D.A. flirt with you and looked the other way. What else do you want from me?"

She started the engine. "Nick, there's nothing between me and Jack Winter except mutual loathing."

"Right. That's why he looks at you like you're an appetizer."

"I think you're making too much of it."

"Am I?"

Sharyn held the steering wheel tightly. "I don't know what to say."

They drove in silence until they reached the sleazy motel parking lot. Sharyn shut off the engine but held the steering wheel.

Nick reached across the seat between them and pried her hand from its death grip on the wheel. "Say you'll have dinner with me. *Alone.* Say we can talk about something besides dead people and the weather. And don't make up an excuse about the election like you did with Winter or I'll start thinking that all that's between *us* is mutual loathing."

Sharyn looked at him holding her hand. Her heart was racing in her chest and she felt light-headed. "Okay."

"Tonight?"

"Tonight."

"Eight. My apartment. I'll cook for you."

Ed was walking towards the Jeep. Sharyn was nervous about him seeing Nick holding her hand. "Okay."

"Good."

She snatched her hand away from him and scooted out of the Jeep as if it was on fire. Nick sat back against the seat and briefly closed his eyes. *Yes! I've finally done it!*

"Sheriff?" Ed glanced at Nick in the Jeep. "Are you two arguing again?"

Sharyn shook her head. "No. What's up?"

Joe had already taped off the area with yellow crime scene tape. It wasn't unusual to see the tape at the motel beside the old bridge. For some reason, it got more than its share of Diamond Springs' crime.

Marti Martin, the owner of the Bridge Motel, was waiting for them. "Sheriff, this is bad for business."

"Mr. Martin." She nodded as she put on her hat. "What happened now?"

"I don't know. The old lady checked in and she

died. End of story. Is everything that happens here a crime? Can't some people just die and that's all there is to it?"

"Some people," she agreed. "What's her name?"

"I'll have to check."

"Please do."

Sharyn followed Nick past the tape and into the tiny closet-sized room. The motel had seen its better days when it was first built by the half-finished bridge back in the fifties. Since then it had gone into a state of steady decline. The rooms were dark and barely maintained. The wind from the lake flapped against a loose shingle and rocked the half-lit neon sign.

Nick pulled out a pair of latex gloves and Joe clapped him on the back. "You come prepared, man!"

"There's no point in coming any other way," Nick replied, walking carefully into the room.

Sharyn glanced around, seeing the lack of personal items. There was no luggage, no purse. Nothing on the nightstand by the bed. The old lady was laid out on her pillows neatly. Not a single hair was out of place.

Marti Martin came to the door but wouldn't come into the room. "I hate dead bodies!"

"You live in the wrong place then," Sharyn told him. "What's her name?"

"Eleanor Roosevelt."

Nick stopped what he was doing and glared at the man. "What?"

"You heard me." Marti shrugged. "I had no reason to doubt her. If somebody says they're Eleanor Roosevelt, then—"

"When did she check in?" Sharyn asked him.

"About a week ago."

"Does one of those cars out there belong to her?" Joe asked him.

"No. She said she came by bus."

"Did she say where she was from?"

"Someplace out west, I think." Marti squirmed. "Can I go now?"

"Yeah, let's talk about it out here, Marti," Joe said, leading the man back outside.

"Well?" Ed wondered, watching Nick.

Nick was drawing back the blanket and sheet that covered the woman. "If she was killed, the murderer was extremely careful. Look at her! She looks like she's sleeping."

THREE

"THIS ROOM IS a mess," Sharyn said, noting the broken lamp on the floor, the smashed lampshade, and the overturned chairs. "And there's nothing personal. Did you find anything in here at all?"

Ed shook his head. "Not a thing."

"Well, the woman definitely had a pocketbook," Sharyn decided. "And a suitcase. *Someone* took them."

"This might be some pill residue on this side table," Nick added, inspecting the white powder on the cracked tabletop. "We'll go over it. There're three things I see right away—her hands, her throat and her eyes."

Sharyn walked closer to the woman. "What about them?"

Nick pointed to the woman's hands. "There was a ring on each hand for a long time. One was the wedding band position. They're both gone."

Sharyn took notes and looked up.

"Then her throat. There're some markings on her throat. No bruising, so we know it happened after she was dead. She was probably wearing a necklace of some sort and the thief took it after she died."

"Could they be ligature marks? Was she strangled?" Sharyn asked.

"I don't think so. They aren't really deep enough for the force it would take to strangle her. And no bruising. I think it was an afterthought. It was probably jerked from her throat."

"So you think she was killed and then robbed?"

"Probably." Nick shrugged. "I'll know more when I do the autopsy. She's been dead for a while. Maybe twenty-four hours or more. Look at her eyes, Sharyn."

Sharyn looked at the woman more closely. "Ruptured blood vessels."

"She may have been suffocated," Nick surmised. "Possibly with that extra pillow."

"Did you get pictures?" she asked Ed.

He nodded. "Joe took some. It's almost like she knew she was going to be robbed."

"Why?" Sharyn looked at him.

"Why else wouldn't she give her real name? Maybe she was trying to protect herself."

"Probably for the same reason most people who stay here don't give their real names. Everyone here has something to hide."

"I figure she's somewhere in her late fifties, maybe early sixties." Nick looked at her hair. "I think we're looking at new hair growth here."

"What would that mean?" Ed wondered.

"Maybe a cancer patient undergoing chemotherapy."

"What a way to end it," Ed said with a shake of his head.

"I need to get everything over here," Nick said slowly. "And I'll need some time with her."

"You're the M.E.," Ed told him.

"I'll call for you," Sharyn volunteered. "I've got you on speed dial."

Nick grimaced. "With the way things are going around here, that's a smart idea."

Sharyn told Keith and Megan that there might have been another homicide. She glanced at her watch. "I have to go, Nick. But I'll leave Joe and Ed with you. David and JP should be coming on duty soon."

"Off to another political rally?" he guessed.

"Yes. Keep me posted, huh?"

"You got it. Eight o'clock?"

She glanced at Ed, but he was preoccupied with the murder scene. "Eight o'clock."

She spoke with Ed and Joe briefly about making sure Marti Martin understood that the room had to be sealed.

"I would think he'd know the procedure by now," Joe replied. "But I'll remind him. He's going to check into how Ms. Roosevelt paid for her room."

"Great. Let me know if anything turns up. Let's do

a quick perimeter check just in case. Maybe someone in another room heard something or saw someone. If nothing else, we know this woman was robbed."

"Good luck at the rally," Ed offered with a dimpled smile.

"Thanks. I'm going to be there with Roy, so I'll need it."

"Debate?" Joe queried.

"Not exactly. Just answering questions together on our different viewpoints."

"I'll look for the sound bites on the news tonight!" he said, laughing.

Sharyn drove back to the office to change clothes. Don wanted her to wear her dress uniform to the program. It was amazing how, one day, men were intimidated by her uniform and the next she was expected to wear it. She couldn't keep up. But she'd promised the party that she'd try. They'd called him a "brilliant political strategist." She just hoped he was brilliant at politics in Diamond Springs.

TRUDY WAS LOOKING particularly grim when she walked in the door. She hadn't been her normal cheerful self since her husband, Ben, had died in a fiery crash out at the motor speedway about six months ago, but this was bad even for her.

"What's wrong, Trudy?" Sharyn asked her quietly, hoping nothing else had gone wrong.

"Ernie had to go out on a call."

Sharyn nodded. "Is he okay? What happened?"

"I don't know how to tell you this, Sheriff, but—"

Ernie walked through the back door holding a prisoner's arm, his expression troubled.

"Kristie?" Sharyn called her sister's name even as she saw that Ernie had her in handcuffs and was dragging her along with him.

"It's your sister," Trudy finished with a sigh. "She was picked up for shoplifting at the mall."

"Shoplifting what?" Sharyn asked, although her brain wasn't connected fully to her mouth. *Kristie? Shoplifting?*

"A few CD's from the big music store."

Sharyn launched herself towards the conference room where Ernie was taking her sister. She glared at him as he sat Kristie down in a hard wooden chair, but didn't take the cuffs off of her.

"Why is she in cuffs?" Sharyn demanded as he walked out of the room. "What's going on?"

"Out here," Ernie directed her as he closed the conference room door on Kristie's defiant face.

"Ernie—"

"Sheriff, she got caught stealing five CD's. She didn't even try to deny it. The manager called your house for someone to pick her up, and no one answered so he called here. When I got there, she wouldn't come with me. A security guard had to hold her down and I put the cuffs on her."

Sharyn bit her lip. "I'm sorry, Ernie."

"I had no choice," he whispered in an anguished voice. He put one arm around her shoulder. "You know I love her like my own daughter. But I couldn't control her. She simmered down a little in the car, but she won't talk to me."

"Are they going to press charges?"

He nodded. "They want her locked up as an example."

Her eyes were bright on his thin face. "Did you tell them she's my sister?"

"I didn't have to," he answered. "She'd already made that clear. She threatened the manager with that."

"What?"

"She told him that you'd come down there and close his store if he didn't let her go."

Sharyn digested the information quickly. "Will you call my mother?"

Ernie balked. It was rare for him to question her judgment but she wasn't just the sheriff on this one. "I think you should let me talk to her."

"I want to talk to her, Ernie."

"As her big sister? Or as the sheriff?"

Sharyn glanced up at him as she put her hand on

the doorknob. "Both." She stepped into the room and closed the door firmly behind her.

"Go ahead," Kristie said without interest. "Tell me that I was way out of line. Tell me that I've ruined my life. I don't care."

Sharyn didn't sit down at the scarred wooden table. She tried hard to figure out what her father would have said if he'd been faced with this situation. Somehow his words wouldn't come. There was only Kristie and her.

"I know you had the money for those CD's," she began. "So I guess you did this to strike out—"

"It's always about you, isn't it, Sharyn? You're always right. You're always perfect. Daddy's little girl turned big bad sheriff! You can do it all, can't you? A house falls in on you, and you just look the other way and limp back to work! Why can't we all be big and strong like Sharyn?"

Kristie's newly pierced lip was swollen. Her voice was lisping and difficult to understand. Sharyn knew it hurt to throw the words at her.

"I was going to say that I thought you were striking out at the world because it let this happen to you."

"This?" Kristie pushed back her shirt with her cuffed hands so that the ugly two-inch scar was exposed on her neck. There was a smaller one on her hand and another on her arm where one of the demons from Bell's Creek had cut her, thinking that

she was a woman from another lifetime. He'd almost killed her. "Just *this?* Why should it matter? I should have been able to get back on my feet. But I'm not like you, Sharyn! I'm not made of grit and nails. I bleed and I hurt. And I almost died."

"I know this isn't just because of that scar or the experience. Maybe it started with Dad being killed, I don't know." Sharyn sat down wearily in one of the chairs. "I know you don't want my help, Kristie. I know you hate me right now. But understand this. Right now, you're on your way to jail. The manager of that store wants to press charges against you. Going to jail won't make you feel any better."

"I don't care," Kristie replied coldly. "I don't care about any of it."

Sharyn smiled. "You know, you were always everything I wanted to be."

Her sister snorted. "Like what? A *cheerleader?*"

"Yes. Like a *cheerleader.* And a straight-A student. And beautiful and popular. And all those things you are that I'm not."

"Those things never meant anything to you." Kristie refused to believe her. "You're strong and brave and able to leap tall buildings in a single bound. Super sheriff."

Two pairs of blue eyes so identical there could be no denying that these two women were sisters, met across the table. Nothing else about them was similar.

Sharyn was tall and large-boned and square-faced. Kristie was slender and petite, as dainty as china.

"I was never so terrified as when I saw that madman trying to kill you," Sharyn confessed. "I was so weak I could hardly stand. I couldn't breathe. I've thought a hundred times that I might not have had to kill that man to save you. But at the time, I did what I could."

Tears were slipping down Kristie's pretty cheeks. "Sharyn, I—I don't know what to do. I can't sleep. I can't eat. When I close my eyes, I see him again and I feel that knife cutting me. I wake up and look at this scar and I know my life is over. My *whole* life! I know I won't ever be able to do those things that I dreamed about doing. It can never be the same."

Sharyn held Kristie and they wept together. Selma came in with Ernie and they found them that way.

"I came as soon as I could," Selma said breathlessly. "Faye just wasn't able."

Sharyn unlocked Kristie's handcuffs and gave them to Ernie. "You're an adult, Kristie. I can't release you. Not while there are charges pending against you. I'll go and talk to the manager of the store. Aunt Selma will stay with you until I get back."

"Thanks, Sharyn," Kristie whimpered. "I'm so sorry."

Ernie nodded. "We won't process anything until we hear from you."

"Thanks." Sharyn sniffed and wiped at her eyes. "I'll be back as soon as I can."

Don James was waiting outside the conference room. "You look awful, Sheriff! And they've started the rally without you. What's wrong? Where's your dress uniform?"

"I'm not going to make the rally," Sharyn said harshly. "There's something I have to do."

As she was walking out of the back door to the office, she heard Foster Odom rushing in through the front door. "Where's the sheriff? Will she comment on her sister's arrest for shoplifting?"

IT WAS LATE when Sharyn got back from Macie's Music store in the new mall up on the interstate. Aunt Selma was sitting upright in a chair with Kristie's head in her lap. The girl was resting on two chairs, sound asleep.

"Well?" Selma asked quietly.

Sharyn nodded. "He's willing to drop the charges. I paid for the CD's and the security guard time. She can't ever go back there or the charges will come up again."

Selma closed her eyes and breathed a silent prayer. "Well done!"

Sharyn sat down at the old table. "I hope it's for the best. Maybe I should have let her take the brunt of it, Aunt Selma. How else is she going to learn?"

"Not behind bars in the county jail, Sharyn! I'm going to take her home with me for a while. Your mother is going through this thing with Caison, and you're running around for this election. Kristie needs some extra attention. I can give her that."

"Thanks." Sharyn let out a pent-up breath. "I used my position as sheriff to get Kristie off, Aunt Selma. I didn't do that when you were in trouble."

Selma held her head high. "You couldn't help me, Sharyn. Not like you could help Kristie. And I shouldn't have asked you. Besides, you made it better anyway."

"It worked out, but—"

"Don't think about it again! And for what's it's it's worth, I've known parents who've done what you just did! The store manager didn't drop the charges just because you were the sheriff. He dropped the charges because you were there and you care about your sister. Faye should have been there instead of you."

"Thanks." Sharyn smiled. She glanced at her watch. It was seven forty-five. *Nick!*

"I think you should go, Sharyn," her aunt said, as though reading her mind. "Let me handle your sister."

Sharyn looked at Kristie's sleeping face, her swollen lip and purple hair. "All right. Tell me if you need anything."

"I will, but I think she just needs some time."

"I love you, Aunt Selma," Sharyn said, hugging the other woman. "Thanks."

"I love you, too, honey. Go home. Get a good night's sleep. Kristie will get better."

Sharyn got in her Jeep, debating if she should go to Nick's or go home. She had her cell phone in her hand and started to dial his number three times and hung up. The last time, he'd actually answered.

It had been an emotionally grueling day. She was exhausted. She was still wearing her uniform, and she didn't feel like eating anything. She just wanted to be alone in a dark room and have a good cry, though it was stupid and weak and wouldn't do anyone a bit of good. Besides, she wasn't a crybaby.

But she knew she wasn't fit to be anyone's company that night, either. She dialed Nick's number one last time.

"Hello?"

"Nick."

"Sharyn? Was that you before?"

"Yes."

"Did something come up?"

She reached his apartment building and looked up at the lighted window that she knew was his. "Yes. I—I just can't make it tonight, Nick."

There was a long pause on the line. "Where are you, Sharyn?"

She looked around. "In your parking lot."

"Stay right there."

It seemed that she had no sooner clicked off her cell phone than he was there. He leaned in the car window. "Still in your uniform?"

She nodded.

He opened the door. "Walk with me?"

Sharyn put her hand in his and let him lead her down to a lighted path by the lake. The sun was setting behind them, throwing shafts of orange light across the lake's mirrored surface. Colored lights reflected the houses on the shore. A few boats were out for night cruises.

"Have you ever wondered why things happen?" he asked her finally as they walked through a stand of old pines.

She breathed in the scent of the trees and the water. From somewhere in the evening twilight, the smell of grilling food floated on the breeze. "All the time."

"I joined the Navy because my father and my grandfather were in the Navy, and I wanted them to be proud of me. I never told anyone that I was scared of the water. I knew they wouldn't believe it. But if I hadn't joined the Navy, I wouldn't have become a doctor. I wouldn't have become a medical examiner. I probably wouldn't have ended up here."

"Sometimes it must seem like that would have been for the best," she murmured.

He stopped walking and squeezed her hand. "Not for a long time."

She looked up into his face. Her heart was pounding in her chest and her face felt hot. "Nick, I—"

"Do you remember what happened that night in the hospital? After you were hurt at the campground?"

She swallowed hard. Her mouth was dry and her tongue refused to work for a moment. "Yes. You— you kissed me. At least I thought you—I might have imagined it. They'd given me stuff. I was—"

"I kissed you," he confirmed, grateful to have those words out between them.

She shrugged. "It was a very emotional time. I know you were worried. *I* was scared. Things can happen—"

They were standing very close. It didn't take much. He bent his head quickly and laid his mouth on hers. His lips were cool and firm and tasted like mint.

Nick didn't let go of her hand. Instead he drew her nearer, sighing deeply when he held her close and she didn't move away. "Well, Sheriff Sharyn Howard, what now?"

"Now." She drew a ragged breath and relaxed against him. "Now I find a diplomatic way to tell you that this will never work and that it would be a bad idea for the county medical examiner and the sheriff to date each other."

"To which I add, you will never convince me of

that. I've known you too long, and I feel like I've waited forever for this moment."

Sharyn lifted her head from his shoulder and smiled at him. "I suppose we *could* have dinner."

Nick nodded. "Dinner would be a good place to start."

They started walking back towards the apartment building. Nick kept his arm around her shoulders, hugging her close.

"You know, I've never been in a relationship with a man for longer than two weeks," she confessed, feeling suddenly very lighthearted.

"Really?" He was amazed. "That long, huh? I think my record is two dates."

Sharyn laughed. "But I've already seen your apartment and your office."

He paused and kissed her parted lips. "Then we'll have to try for three, won't we?"

"Good morning everyone, and welcome to another homicide in Diamond Springs!" Nick's voice was darkly jovial about the subject. He looked up as he set his briefcase down on the conference table in the sheriff's office. "Where's the sheriff?"

David and JP were still there from nightshift, yawning and chugging down coffee. Ed was doodling hearts and pretty girls' faces while Cari watched him and tried not to notice David scowling at her across the table.

Joe was eating one of the cinnamon rolls that Trudy had brought them. He shrugged. "Not here?"

"Yes, I noticed that. Ernie's gone, too. Was there an emergency that I didn't hear about, besides the murder?"

Ed groaned. "Couldn't we just pretend that old woman died of natural causes, Nick? One murder in two or three years used to be a lot around here. Two or three in a year is too much!"

"I'd like to oblige, but the county frowns on me doing autopsies for no reason," Nick told him, taking out his papers.

Ernie joined them in the conference room. "Morning, Nick."

"What's up this morning?"

"You didn't hear?"

"I guess not," Nick replied, a cold stab of fear in his heart. "Is it Sharyn?"

"Kristie was picked up for shoplifting last night." Everyone shook their heads.

"What happened at the store?" Cari asked.

"Sharyn managed to convince the manager to drop the charges," Ernie told them. "Kristie went home with Selma."

"I saw part of it on the six o'clock news last night,"

Ed muttered. "It's not gonna look good that she got the charges dropped."

"Maybe not." Sharyn entered the room and closed the door behind her. "But I didn't promise any special favors, and I didn't lean on him. I paid for the CD's Kristie took and the security guards' wages who were there with her."

"You know, I didn't think anything of it, Sheriff," Ed replied. "I just know how these things look."

"Especially in an election year," David added somberly.

"Yeah, like it would hurt your feelings if she lost," Joe pounced on him.

"I work with her, too," David yelled back.

"Settle down!" Sharyn demanded. "We're not going to worry about the election right now. It seems that we have another homicide on our hands. I think we should do our jobs and let everything else take care of itself."

Nick shook his head and finished taking out the documents he'd brought with him. "Joe and Ed found Jane Doe at the Bridge Motel yesterday. There are no fingerprints on record for her, which only means she didn't serve in the military and wasn't a criminal. She was about fifty-five or sixty years old, about one hundred and ten pounds, five foot six. Caucasian, blue eyes, and probably had chemotherapy recently."

"How could you tell that?" David asked.

"New hair growth, and, after the internal exam, trace amounts of fluorouracil still in her body. There was massive cancer damage to her liver and pancreas. If she hadn't been murdered, I would've only given her a few days to survive at best. The woman must have been going on sheer willpower."

"But you're sure she was murdered, Nick?" Ed asked, glancing around the table. "I mean, if she was that near death anyway. Maybe it was an accident."

Nick nodded. "She was killed. Actually, she was suffocated with her pillow. Her saliva, sweat and skin cells were on the pillow beside her. But she didn't fight her attacker. No broken fingernails. In fact, no bruising around the mouth and nose, which gives you an idea of how easy it was to kill her. She was killed about twenty-four hours before we found her."

"No way!" Joe protested. "She was as calm on that bed as if she just went to sleep! Why wouldn't she have fought if she were suffocated? Isn't that instinctive?"

"It's my opinion that she was very near death at the time," Nick answered. "The struggle was already past for her. She was on heavy painkillers. There were traces of Dilaudid on her hands and a bottle on the bedside table. She was loaded up with it. It's a common painkiller for end-stage cancer. But, regardless of her health, she *was* suffocated. This wasn't a natural death."

"So somebody suffocated then robbed a dying woman?" JP questioned, shaking his dark head. "I cannot believe anyone could be so heartless."

"Well, they probably didn't know she was almost dead," Nick consoled him. "There were marks on the sides of her neck and on both of her hands. I think she was wearing two rings and a chain around her throat. The thief took everything. She has nothing to identify her."

"Maybe if she was someone's patient, she's missing from a hospital," Sharyn suggested, looking at Nick's notes.

"That's a possibility," he agreed. "My scenario on this is that someone broke into the room she was in. She probably woke up before they got what they wanted, so she was eliminated."

"If that's what happened," Joe reported, "no one saw or heard any of it at the motel."

"That's harsh," David said.

"But why was she here?" Sharyn asked aloud, looking at the photo of the dead woman. "It was all she had, but her nightgown was nice and new-looking. Her hands were well cared for. She looked clean. She wasn't a homeless person looking for a place to die."

"We probably won't know that until we find out who she is," Nick said quietly.

"And why give an obvious fake name if she wasn't hiding from someone?" Cari added.

"If she'd escaped from a hospital and wanted to die alone in a small, dingy motel, she might have been afraid someone would look for her," Joe surmised.

"Well, I suppose the place to start would be to check out the internet and see if anyone's reported a cancer patient missing in the past few days," Ernie said. "If she was as bad off as you say, Nick, she couldn't have been from too far out West like Martin claimed. She wouldn't have been able to take the trip."

"I'll help you, Ernie." Cari joined him. "I still have a ton of those musket people to enter into the computer anyway."

"That's good," Sharyn agreed. "Ed, you and Joe take patrol. See if you can roust out some local thieves who might have done this. I don't think it was well-planned. The woman may have been trying to hide, but the thieves were messy. I don't think they were stalking her."

"I've got some fingerprints from the pillowcase besides the massive amount of prints all over the room to check out," Nick offered. "Maybe someone else will show up."

"It seems like there should have been more drugs of some kind on the scene if this woman was so ill," Cari told them. "When my grandmother died last year from cancer, she was taking about ten different medications just to stay alive."

"That's a good angle," Sharyn commended. "Thanks, Cari. Let's check that lead out, too. We probably know some buyers who might want those drugs."

"Do you need us, Sheriff?" David asked, yawning.

"No. I just wanted you to be aware of the situation. If I need you, I'll call. Go home and get some sleep. Thanks for staying a little longer, David, JP."

JP Santiago smiled. His broad, pleasant face looked grim. "Always glad to help, Sheriff. This is a terrible crime. I want to see this person caught."

"Me, too. How's that new baby?"

"Luci is well, thank you. We would be honored if you, all of you, could come to her christening next week."

"Just let us know when, JP," Sharyn told him with a smile. "I wouldn't miss it."

David gave Cari a mutinous look that she purposely missed while she was gathering her papers together. She walked out of the conference room with Ernie, leaving Joe and Ed to follow.

"David," Ed began, only to have his nephew turn away from him.

"Leave me alone."

Nick was packing his briefcase, glancing up when

he and Sharyn were alone together in the room. "Why didn't you tell me about Kristie last night?"

"What good would it do?"

He ran his hand through his hair. "It's part of having a relationship, Sharyn. You tell me things. I tell you things."

"I told you I wasn't very good at this."

"I'm not, either," he admitted. "But maybe we could both be better?"

Sharyn shook her head with a nervous glance at the outer office to see if anyone was paying them any attention. "Nick, maybe this isn't such a good idea."

"Come on! We haven't even made it to the second date yet!"

"I know." She smiled at him hesitantly. "Okay. I didn't think about it like that. I'll try to tell you things."

"Like when your sister gets arrested for shoplifting or you get shot," he suggested. "Important things."

"Okay." She watched him come closer to her, then she stepped away from him.

"Sharyn?"

"Nick! We're in the middle of the office! How would it look for you to—"

"Sheriff?" Trudy glanced between them with a satisfied smile on her face. "There's a man out near the mill who thinks he may have found the senator's car in the woods near his house."

Sharyn nodded. "Thanks, Trudy. I'll go and take a look."

"Sure." Trudy grinned and left them alone.

"I don't think we're going to be able to talk about this right now, but we're going to have to establish some guidelines, if we're going to have a relationship," Nick said slowly.

Sharyn searched his face carefully. "Are we going to have a relationship, Nick?"

His gaze touched her lips. "Yes, Sharyn. I think we are. Let's establish the rest of this on date number two. Does that work for you?"

"Yes. Thanks."

"Sure. I have to get to work."

"Me, too. Bye, Nick."

He shook his head awkwardly and stalked out of the building.

"What do you think of *that?*" Trudy asked, nudging Ernie as he was trying to pour coffee into his cup.

Ernie grabbed a paper towel. "I think I could be seriously burned while you're trying to point whatever it is out to me."

"Nick and Sharyn! Didn't you see the way they were looking at each other?"

He shrugged and took a sip of his coffee. "I didn't see anything unusual, Trudy."

"Ernie, that computer work will have to wait,"

Sharyn told him as she grabbed her gun and hat. "I want you to come out to look at this car with me."

"Yes, ma'am!"

"That's not fair," Cari moaned. "I want to go out in the field!"

"When you're trained, young'un," Ernie told her, picking up his own hat and gun. "In the meantime, dazzle us with what you can find out about Jane Doe."

"Sure." She sighed.

"Hi, Charlie." Sharyn turned to the retired deputy who'd come in for a cup of coffee. "How's it going?"

"Fine, Sheriff. We had a little trouble with one of the dogs last night, but he'll be fine."

"I can't believe that man wants to keep on working," Ernie said as they were getting into Sharyn's Jeep. "And I *really* can't believe you have him out here doing the surveillance cameras and taking care of the dogs!"

She shrugged. "Some people want to sit on their porches watching the cars go by when they retire. Some don't. There must be room for both."

He grinned at her with his half grin. "There is while you're sheriff, anyway."

"That's right. And I mean to keep it that way!"

FOUR

Mr. Foyle Duke was waiting for them on the side of the road. He pulled at his Atlanta Braves baseball cap when Sharyn introduced herself and Ernie.

"I was cutting down some hay when I noticed the car back in the woods," he told them. "I wouldn't have thought to call you but for that mess with the senator. I heard you couldn't find his car."

"That's right," Ernie said. "You haven't seen the car back there before?"

"Nope. Somebody ran down some hay to get it there, too. There were fresh tracks to the woods."

"Okay," Sharyn decided. "Let's go and take a look."

Mr. Duke took them through the newly mown field on his tractor. His property was only about a mile from the old mill, off a back road that was rarely used. Sharyn knew it was the senator's car as soon as she saw it.

"Somebody sure made a mess of it," Mr. Duke remarked, spitting tobacco on the ground.

"Looks like a sledgehammer, maybe," Ernie considered, taking pictures of the crushed silver Lincoln.

"Why park here?" Sharyn asked quietly.

"Maybe it wasn't the senator."

"That's possible," she admitted. "There could be prints."

"No footprints on the ground, though, after the storms we've had since then."

"Too bad, huh? But maybe we'll get something from the inside."

Sharyn walked around the badly mangled car. The fenders had been crushed, the windows smashed out. The tires were all slit. There was no way to disguise the fact that it was the senator's car by what had been done to it. She had to assume it was pure rage.

"Thanks, Mr. Duke," she said, shaking the man's dirty hand. "We'll arrange for someone to come and get it so we can take a look at it."

"Sure thing. Thanks for comin', Sheriff."

"You have to be thinking what I'm thinking about all that," Ernie said as they got back into the Jeep.

"Anger. Spite. There wouldn't be any other reason for it."

"Still, whoever it was thought about taking the car somewhere else."

"*If* that person shot the senator. Caison might have driven it here himself. I have a hard time envisioning him at the mill thinking about his childhood. He was out here for a reason and he doesn't want us to know what it was."

"Or someone stole the car after the senator left it at the mill," Ernie elaborated.

She agreed. "That's possible, I suppose. The car being here might not be connected at all."

"We checked out the reenactors pretty well," Ernie supplied. "Only a few know how to use a musket, and none of them had musket balls on them. There was only one musket that was loaded for demonstrations, and it was still loaded."

"Anyone who'd been at the festival in the last three days could have seen the one that was loaded for the demo. He could have arranged to meet the senator at the mill, they argued, he took his best shot. He knew the senator would keep his mouth closed and look for his own way of getting back at him."

"I didn't see where the car was forcibly started," Ernie remarked. "The senator must have left his keys in the ignition."

Sharyn nodded. "He's not used to driving himself anywhere."

Ernie agreed. "We should know something after Nick's kids climb all over it anyway."

"Sheriff," Trudy's voice squawked on the radio. "Ed and Joe have another situation down at the Bridge Motel. They think they have the Jane Doe thief holed up in a motel room. They've requested a search warrant. It's on its way."

"Thanks, Trudy," Ernie said. "Looks like it's going to be a busy week."

"You don't know the half of it," Sharyn replied, taking the Jeep on the interstate to reach Diamond Springs faster.

Ernie glanced at her sideways. "I'm a quick study if someone tells me."

Sharyn opened her mouth to speak, then shook her head. It was all too new. "I can't tell you right now, Ernie."

He frowned. "Is it something bad?"

"I don't know," she admitted. "I guess we'll have to wait and see."

"Sharyn—"

"*Now* you call me Sharyn!"

"*Sharyn,*" he continued, "if you need someone to talk to, I'm always here for you."

"I know." She smiled. "But this is something… *strange.*"

"Well, strange or not, it can't be stranger than what I told you about that whole thing at Jefferson. You can trust me."

"I know, Ernie. I just can't tell anyone yet."

Ernie sat back in his seat with a satisfied smirk on his thin face. *Trudy was right! Something else had happened. How had he missed it?* "I'm just gonna call in for the flatbed to pick up the senator's car."

"Okay."

They pulled into the motel parking lot. Ed waved to them.

"We got him cornered in room number six," Joe told them with his gun drawn.

"Is he armed?" Sharyn asked him.

"Maybe. Marti called us. He recognized the man as having been around here the past few days but he didn't have the money for a room. Now he has the money. Marti said Jane Doe paid for her room with cash and had a wad of it besides."

Sharyn surveyed the scene. The room was situated to the back of the motel, almost against the old bridge pylons. There was one small window in the front and only one door to get in. If they went up there with their guns drawn, it could mean a firefight. They could lose the suspect and possibly any hope of finding out who Jane Doe was, besides running the risk that one of them could be injured.

"If we don't know that he's armed, let's not spook him," she decided. "I'll pick up some sheets from Marti and maybe we can get in without any guns."

Ed scratched his head. "I don't see the plan here, Sheriff. You're gonna dress up like a ghost and pretend it's Halloween already?"

Sharyn laughed. "I'm going to pretend to be the maid. You stay put and get ready."

"Sheriff!" Ernie whispered loudly with a worried

eye on the door to the number six room. "I don't know—"

"You watch the door. If we can get it open without alarming him, we stand a better chance of no one getting hurt."

Sharyn found some clean sheets and towels in the main office. She also found a blue smock. She pulled it on over her uniform and picked up a big bundle of sheets and towels, holding it in front of her.

"Sheriff! I just got those washed!" Marti protested.

"If you paid someone to do it," she grimaced, thinking about sleeping on them, "you paid too much!"

Joe, Ed, and Ernie were all out of sight when she left the office. She hid her gun inside one of the towels she was carrying. If she could manage to get the door open and get inside without the suspect realizing what was going on, they would all be better off.

"I hope this is a good idea," Ed said, biting his fingernail as he watched her knock on the motel room door.

"She's the sheriff," Ernie explained rationally. "She made the call."

"Yeah, well it won't look good for the rest of us if the sheriff is shot while she's running for reelection."

"Not for us," Joe confided, "but it'll look good for *her!*"

Ernie glared at him. "She doesn't have to win that way."

"I know that," Joe answered. "Maybe he's not in there anyway."

Sharyn knocked again, more loudly this time. There was no response. She waited again then pounded on the door. "Maid! I gotta change those sheets!"

The door opened slowly. "Yeah?"

"Clean towels and sheets," Sharyn said.

"I didn't ask for any," the man said still standing just inside the doorway.

Sharyn could only see his rough black shoes and ragged pants. She raised her gaze and saw that his hands were empty. He was wearing a greasy white T-shirt and no belt. There was no weapon on him anywhere that she could see.

"Fine. You can just take these then. I can go home early."

The man stepped forward to take the sheets and towels from her. Quickly, before he could move back inside the room, she shoved the towels and sheets at him, knocking him to the floor. Joe and Ernie were on him before he could get to his feet or look at who'd been carrying the towels.

"What? What'd I do?"

"We want to talk to you about your sudden good

fortune," Joe told him as he pulled him up from the floor.

"What sudden good fortune? I don't know what you're talking about!"

"We're talking about a murder that happened here early Sunday morning." Ernie glanced at the man's wallet. "Willy? Is that you?"

"I don't know nothing about no murder, Deputy! You got the wrong guy!"

"We'll see," Joe said, searching him. "Got a gun?"

"No," Willy replied. "Well, not on me. I got one in the room but that's not against the law!"

"Is it registered?" Joe asked.

"No. This is a free country!"

Ernie looked closer at his ID. "This license expired four years ago, Willy."

"No point in renewing it, I ain't got a car to drive."

Sharyn took off the blue smock and looked at the license. "Willy Newsome? Is that your name?"

"Yeah. Hey, watch my arms!"

Ernie held him still while Joe finished searching him.

"He's clean," Joe declared. "But what's this?"

He pulled a thin gold chain from the man's pocket. Attached to it was a small, gold, heart-shaped locket. Ed stepped forward with gloves on his hands to take it from him.

"I think we should take a ride to the sheriff's office, Willy," Ernic told him.

"Am I under arrest?"

"Nope. Not yet at least. But I think we need to have a talk."

"Where'd you get this high-quality luggage, Willy?" Ernie asked, looking at the two blue suitcases.

"I found it."

"Where?"

"In the Dumpster."

"Let's go." Joe pushed his head down to get him into the back of the squad car.

"Don't you have to read me my rights?" Willy demanded. "When do I get my phone call?"

"Not until we arrest you," Joe told him. "We'll tell you when."

Sharyn was on the phone with Nick, telling him about the room he needed to go over. "Ernie and I will wait for you."

"Meet you back at the office," Joe said, getting behind the wheel of the squad car.

Ernie and Sharyn began to go through the things in the dismal motel room. There were food delivery boxes and old pizza all over the room. Empty beer bottles cluttered the floor. The bed was filthy. Sharyn was glad she was wearing gloves, to protect herself as much as the evidence.

Ernie found two women's rings, one a wedding band, on the sink in the bathroom. "I don't think there's much doubt that this is our man."

"He had some kind of fire in here," Sharyn said, looking at the ashes in a metal trash can. "It looks like pictures of some sort."

"Maybe Jane Doe had photos with her. Maybe he thought he could protect himself by getting rid of them."

Sharyn opened up the first suitcase. It was filled with women's clothing about the size Jane Doe was wearing. The second suitcase was filled with prescription drugs and underwear. She picked up one of the brown bottles. "Edith Randolph, 26 East Warren Street, Chadron, Nebraska. Dr. Nym Paddah."

Ernie stopped looking through the drawers in the chest under the television. "Jane Doe?"

"I think so."

They had bagged and labeled most of the evidence in the room before Nick arrived with Megan and Keith.

"Looks like you hit the mother lode," he remarked.

"I think this stuff belongs to our Jane Doe," Ernie told him, showing him the rings and the necklace.

"Edith Randolph," Sharyn added. "Cari was right—she did travel with her own pharmacy."

"She came all the way from Nebraska to die here?"

Nick questioned, taking one of the bottles of medication from Sharyn.

"Apparently."

"I knew this was a popular place," Megan announced to no one in particular, "but I don't think I'd travel halfway across the country for it!"

"We have to go and have a talk with Willy Newsome, the man we found here with her stuff," Sharyn told Nick as she stripped off her gloves. "Let me know as soon as you can confirm that this stuff is Jane Doe's. That will give us enough to hold him until we can decide if he killed her."

He nodded. "I have some evidence from the top of the pillow that should link him to the crime without any doubt. If he pressed it into her face, we'll know it."

"Great." She looked up at him. "Thanks, Nick."

He smiled slowly at her. His eyes lingered on hers. "Anytime, Sheriff."

Sharyn's heart skipped a beat. She turned away. "Sheriff?" Keith caught her as she was walking out the door. "I heard about Kristie. Is there any chance I could see her?"

"Only if she calls you, Keith," Sharyn replied, not wanting to be cold, but not wanting to encourage the boy, either.

"Is she at home? I could call her. Maybe she'd want to see me now." He shrugged his shoulders beneath his faded T-shirt. A long strand of his thin hair fell forward and he pushed it back with his glasses.

"Keith." Sharyn put her hand on his shoulder to comfort him. "I know you care for Kristie, but you'll have to let her go through this. We all do."

"I know." He smiled half-heartedly. "Just tell her I asked, huh?"

"I will."

Ernie stripped off his gloves and walked out of the motel with Sharyn. "That was pitiful."

"Now you know how you looked when you and Annie were having problems."

"I didn't look like a little lost puppy," he corrected her.

"Ask Trudy if you don't believe me!"

THEY MET ED, Joe and Cari back at the office. Cari and Ed stayed to help with the prisoner, and Joe and Ernie went home. JP and David had already been called out to handle a marital disturbance on the other side of town.

"Hi, Marvella," Sharyn greeted the cleaning lady. "I haven't seen you in a while."

"No killings, I expect," Marvella answered, her dark face a concerned frown. "Who you got in there now?"

"A man who might be connected to the robbery at the motel."

"Why would any woman stay there alone?" the cleaning lady asked.

"I don't know," Sharyn answered. "Maybe she wasn't alone."

"Poor thing. I read about her in the paper. Eat up with cancer and this man smothers her! What a world!"

"When are you done with school?" Sharyn smiled at the other woman.

"Next year. January. I'm looking forward to it. No more late nights and cleaning floors behind you people! You're pigs!"

"I'll miss you, too," Sharyn said, laughing. "What are you going to do?"

"After taking twenty years to finish high school and college, I'm gonna find myself a cushy job and watch the world go by." Marvella waved her mop at the dark window that faced the street and tossed her black curls.

"Sounds good," Sharyn said. "Maybe there'll be room for me there, too!"

"You're never gonna leave here."

"I might if I don't win the election."

"That man ain't got nothin' on you, sweetheart. Your daddy's spirit is with you. He's gonna take care of you. And that poor little sister of yours, bless her soul!"

Sharyn smiled again. "Thanks, Marvella."

"Go in there and beat that man into confessing now. I won't watch."

Ed shook his head. "She gets worse every day. You ever get the feeling she knows everything that's going on around here?"

"I *do* know everything," Marvella assured him from the broom closet. "And I have ears like a cat!"

"Shouldn't that be like a dog?"

"I don't think so," Marvella corrected him. "A dog's sniffer is good, but his ears aren't as good as a cat's."

"Why do I have these conversations with you?" Ed wondered earnestly, but he had a wide grin on his face.

"Because you know I have superior intelligence," she baited him, pushing at the mass of glossy black ringlets on her head. "You know when you hear the voice of experience!"

"I'm going to go and beat the prisoner now," Sharyn said to him. "Want to come before Marvella makes you look worse?"

"I'm right behind you, Sheriff."

Willy Newsome was sitting at the big wooden table in the conference room. He was staring at Cari, who was sitting at the other end of the table with her hand on her baton. She hadn't been issued a gun yet but she was taut and ready for him to make a move.

Ed put his hand on her shoulder and she jumped a few inches in the air.

"Oh! Ed, it's you!" She looked at Sharyn. "What do you need me to do now, Sheriff?"

"You can take notes, Cari, thanks." Sharyn took a seat close to Willy. "We have your rap sheet, Willy. I think you can guess it's not a pretty picture."

"I've done a few things wrong. But I served my country, too." He glared at Ed. "You serve your country, boy?"

"No, sir," Ed admitted. "But I haven't robbed any homes lately, either."

"Shoplifting, shoplifting. Convenience store robbery. Assault. Burglary. Home break-in. You've spent almost half of your life in prison since you came back from Vietnam." Sharyn read aloud from the computer sheet.

"I didn't say I was proud of what I done." He wiped his nose on his sleeve and Cari winced. "But I ain't killed no one!"

"Well, why don't you tell us how you came to have a dead woman's stuff in your room, Willy?" Ed encouraged him.

Willy glanced at Sharyn. "I got a lawyer."

"We haven't arrested you yet," Ed said with a smile. "Maybe if you can convince us you didn't kill that woman, we won't have to."

"I ain't stupid, Deputy! You're gonna arrest me no

matter what. You didn't bring me down here to give me a bed for the night." He sat back in his chair. "I want a lawyer. I got a right to have a lawyer."

Sharyn shrugged. "Okay. Let's find Mr. Newsome a comfortable cell while we call a lawyer for him."

Willy opened his wallet and pried an old, dirty business card out of it. "You call him. He knows me."

Sharyn took the card and read the name. "Eldeon Percy. I'll give him a call, sir."

"Hope you got some coffee," Willy said in reply.

Ed took Willy downstairs, then confronted Sharyn. "You know Eldeon Percy isn't going to come over for this guy. He's got expensive tastes and clients that can pay for it."

"I know." She shrugged. "But I'm going to give him a call anyway. This should buy us some time until Nick knows if we have anything to hold him on."

Cari yawned. "If you don't mind, Sheriff, I'm going home."

"That's fine," Sharyn replied. "Thanks for staying."

"I'll see you in the morning."

SHE SAT BACK in her father's old chair and put in a call to Eldeon Percy. Mr. Percy was a famous lawyer around Diamond Springs. He was flamboyant and successful at handling his wealthy clients' unfortunate scrapes with the law. He lived in a huge old house overlooking the lake, where he entertained people like Senator Talbot, Todd Vance, the mayor of Diamond Springs, and D.A. Jack Winters. The man was a legend in the courtroom.

But there was no response, of course. Sharyn glanced at the clock on her computer. It was almost midnight. She left a message for Mr. Percy. She didn't expect him to call back, but she had been true to her word. She was flipping through her contact phone numbers, looking for a court-appointed attorney to call in case they arrested Willy.

The office was quiet around her except for the sound of computers humming and Marvella whistling while she worked. A sudden knock on the door made her jump and look up. "Nick!"

"I called your house. Where's Faye?"

"She's there," Sharyn told him. "She probably didn't hear the phone ring."

"Why are you still here?" he asked, sitting down in a chair that faced her desk.

"I was just calling Eldeon Percy for our suspect. Willy won't talk without his lawyer here. Then I was looking for a lawyer who will actually come if he's guilty and we arrest him."

He glanced around the office. "Where's everyone else?"

"Home, I imagine." She yawned. "Tell me you know something good and that's why you're here."

"I know something good and bad."

"Oh, no."

He grinned, putting down a rough preliminary on his findings. "Now you know how I feel when you tell me a case isn't coming together for you and you just *feel* that it's wrong."

Sharyn checked the report. "The stuff we recovered from the motel *did* belong to Edith Randolph?"

"That's right. Her fingerprints are all over everything. The Dilaudid is there. The rings are the right size. So is the chain mark on her neck. I put in a call to the pharmacy on the prescription and to the doctor listed."

Sharyn nodded as she continued to read. "Ernie put in a request for information to the Nebraska police too. We should probably know more in the morning."

"Keep reading," he suggested.

"Willy's fingerprints don't match the top of the pillowcase? Are you sure she was smothered with *that* pillowcase?"

"Positive. You could almost trace the markings of her face in the pillow. Whoever killed her left us two clear handprints. Not fingerprints, unfortunately, but palms. He didn't wear gloves, and Willy's hands would fit inside those prints. The man who killed her had clean hands. There was even some soap residue. Everything Willy touched had dirty prints on it. I don't think he's your killer."

"So, you think he took everything this woman had but he didn't touch her?"

"I think she was dead already and he came into the room and decided to help himself. He probably thought she was sleeping."

Sharyn stared at him in the fluorescent light, thinking that he looked tired. "Nick, are you telling me that two people came into this dying woman's room? One of them murdered her but didn't take anything. The other one stripped her room but didn't hurt her?"

"That's what I'm saying. Although we don't know if the killer took anything or not since it would be impossible to know everything this woman had with her."

"The D.A.'s going to hate this. We can tag Willy for robbing her but not for the killing? The press is going to eat it up."

"Sorry. That's the best I can do unless you want me to plant evidence to convict him."

"That's not what I was suggesting," she replied.

"Then what?"

"Why can't it just be simple sometimes?" she demanded. "Why does it always have to be so complicated?"

Nick got to his feet. "I don't know, Sharyn. I don't make it that way. I just report the facts. Here's another one— I'm going home now."

He'd reached the door when she called him back. "I'm sorry. I didn't mean to snap at you."

Nick turned to face her. "We're both tired. Let's call it a night, huh? There's nothing else we can do until we hear from her doctor and the police."

She nodded and picked up her backpack. "I guess."

He put his hand on hers as she put the report in her backpack. "Sharyn, about this thing."

"This 'thing'?"

"Between us."

"Oh."

He took the backpack from her hands and set it down on the desk. "I don't know if I can pretend anymore."

She swallowed hard and looked into his dark face. "Nick, if you don't—"

He pulled her close to him. "If you tell me the two of us being together might not be such a good idea again, I swear I'll take out an ad in the *Gazette!* 'Sheriff Sharyn Howard and county medical examiner Nick Thomopolis'—"

"Nick!"

He kissed her quickly. "I don't think I can pretend that I don't have *feelings* for you. I've done it for a long time. I don't want to do it anymore."

"People just need some time," she promised. "Everyone will have to get used to the idea that we don't hate each other."

He studied her face. "How much time?"

"I don't know," she fabricated.

"You mean *you* just need more time to get used to the idea," he accused.

"Okay," she agreed. "*I* just need more time."

He nodded. "I can live with that. For a while anyway. On one condition."

"What's that?"

"That we agree that we *do* have a relationship and that we're going to try our best to spend time together, when we can, away from work. Deal?" He stuck out his hand.

She smiled and put hers into it. "Deal."

"A kiss to seal it?" he asked, drawing her closer.

"We haven't even had our second date yet," she reminded him. But she was letting him pull her closer.

"Ahem!" A voice startled them apart.

Sharyn moved back from Nick. "Mr. Percy?"

"You called, Sheriff," the dapper attorney said, flicking an imaginary speck from his faultless white linen suit. "Did you think I wouldn't come?"

Nick stood up straight. "Mr. Percy."

"Dr. Thomopolis." Percy glanced around the empty office. "Where's my client, Sheriff?"

"He's in a holding cell, sir," Sharyn told him. "We have reason to believe that he committed a robbery at the Bridge Motel."

"Do you have evidence that links my client to the robbery?"

"Yes, sir. We do now."

Percy nodded. "I'd like a cup of coffee, Sheriff. And a word with my client."

"You can come in here, sir," Sharyn took him to the conference room. "I'll bring him up."

"Thank you, Sheriff." Percy looked distastefully at the worn wooden chairs. He took out his clean white handkerchief and wiped the chair before he sat down. "Please don't forget my coffee."

"Go home, Nick," Sharyn said as she passed him on the way to the coffeepot. "You look like you're about to pass out."

"I'm not leaving you here alone with him! Where's David and JP?"

"They're out on a call right now but they'll be back. Marvella's here."

"Oh, *Marvella!*"

"I can hear you Dr. *Lovesick* Thomopolis!"

"Great!"

"Marvella—" Sharyn began.

"I'm not saying a word to anyone. I know how to keep my mouth shut!"

Sharyn grimaced as she turned back to Nick. "Anyway, I'll be fine. You can't protect me from my job, Nick. I'm the sheriff."

"I know." He walked to the coffee machine as he

JOYCE & JIM LAVENE

took off his tie and suit coat. He pulled out three foam cups.

"What are you doing?"

"I thought you'd like a cup, too." He glared at her. "You have to have another person take notes and just be in the room. Even I know that, Sheriff Howard. I'm staying put until someone else gets here. Go get Willy."

Sharyn gave up and went downstairs for Willy. If Nick wanted to stay, he was an adult, he could stay. She squashed down hard on the warm, fuzzy feeling she got just knowing that he was staying with her. He was the M.E. and an emergency deputy. He could be called on from time to time to do things for the sheriff's office. It was nothing personal.

"Sheriff, what are you so happy about?" Willy asked as she opened the cell door.

"I'm not happy," she rebuked. "Just doing my job, Mr. Newsome."

"You're humming, Sheriff. Is that part of your job?"

Sharyn stopped humming and escorted him down the dimly lit hall. She was thinking about Nick when Willy pushed hard against her at the top stair. They toppled down the stairs together, the hard concrete beneath the green tile bruising Sharyn's back as she fell, taking the full brunt of his weight.

"Stop, Willy!" She called out as he stepped on her and ran back towards the stairs.

He kept running. She threw herself against him, knocking him to the floor. He took a swing at her, half connected, then grunted as she slammed her fist into his stomach.

He went down, gagging and moaning. Sharyn touched her eye carefully after she'd put her knee on his back and had the handcuffs on him. What had she been thinking about that she hadn't cuffed him? He hadn't seemed like a flight risk, but—

"Okay," she told him, pushing him to his feet. "Let's go!"

Nick saw her face when they reached the top of the stairs. Eldeon Percy was instructing him on how much sugar to put into his white coffee. The lawyer looked at Willy and shook his head.

"Problems, Sheriff?"

"Nothing I couldn't handle, sir," she grunted.

Percy walked past his client. "Come this way, Mr. Newsome. We'll have a talk. Sheriff, we need some privacy."

The door to the conference room closed behind them.

"What happened?" Nick asked, handing her some ice in a paper towel.

Sharyn winced as she put the ice on her eye. "I didn't cuff him. I know it's a rule—don't remind me. I didn't think he was a flight risk." She didn't admit that she had been thinking about *other* things at the time.

"Let me see that." Nick put a hand on her chin and looked at her swollen eye. "You're gonna have a shiner!"

"Good. I guess we'll add assault to robbery. He seemed harmless enough."

"I thought you knew better."

"Don't start, Nick."

"Sheriff," Percy called from the conference room. "I think my client is ready to deal now."

FIVE

NICK JOINED SHARYN with Percy and Willy at the big table in the conference room. It was late and the office was too quiet around them.

Sharyn looked at the man who'd just smacked her in the eye. His hair was greasy and his clothes were filthy and torn. She knew he was an alcoholic and had probably done worse things than try to get away from her. It was hard to believe that he was also a decorated soldier. At one time, this man had been a hero. According to his service record, he had been awarded the Purple Heart and been cited for bravery. What had happened to him?

"I'm listening," she said to the lawyer.

Eldeon Percy smiled at her. He had a peculiar smile that was more a smirk that just tilted the corners of his mouth. It wasn't a pleasant thing to see. "What are you offering for my client's valuable information, Sheriff?"

Sharyn glanced at Nick, who was typing notes of their conversation on his laptop. "I'm not offering anything, Mr. Percy. We have Willy's fingerprints all over the victim's room and her possessions. He had her locket is his pocket. What else can I say?"

"My client is not your killer, Sheriff. I'm sure you're also aware of that fact?"

"Maybe. We don't know that for sure, do we?"

Percy smirked at Nick. "Tell me, Doctor. Just what did you find when you did your examination of the area?"

"I found your client's dirty paw prints on everything, Counselor. He was in the room with that woman. He took her things and probably sold what he could."

"That may be true," Percy continued. "But who killed your victim? I know you want the killer much more than you want this pitiful shell of a man who was only helping himself to the bountiful harvest he'd found."

Sharyn clasped her hands together on the table. "What do you want, Mr. Percy?"

"I want my client released. I want all charges dropped against him."

Sharyn smiled, then winced as it pained the side of her eye. "We know he robbed the victim, sir. He punched me in the eye and tried to escape. He'd better have the name of the killer and his home address to have all charges dropped against him!"

"Sheriff, you barely know the victim's identity. And I know you don't need the publicity of an unsolved murder case right now. No one who's running for reelection wants that. Why, my friend Jack Winter was just telling me how bad that makes *everyone* involved look to the voters."

She shook her head. "I'm not promising anything before I hear what he has to say. My eye is going to be swollen for a few days. I'm not likely to look the other way on this, Mr. Percy."

Percy inclined his head towards his client and whispered something in Willy's ear. Sharyn could hardly believe this perfectionist would even consider being in the same room with Willy. What was up between them?

Willy nodded. "I saw something that night. The night the woman was killed."

"What?"

"I saw a man walk out of the woman's motel room and get in a car. He drove away but he left the door unlocked. I tried it. I didn't think anyone else was in there. I went into the room and took some of her stuff. She didn't move. She looked like she was asleep to me. I was quiet."

"*Some* of her stuff?" Sharyn refuted him.

He shrugged. "Okay. I took everything I saw."

"What time was that?"

"After midnight. He didn't come back while I was there."

"What did he look like? What kind of car was he driving?"

Percy put his hand on Willy's arm. "I think that's enough for now, Willy."

Sharyn glared at him. "If you want me to make these other charges go away, you'd better have something else!"

Percy glared back. "I haven't heard an offer yet."

Nick looked at them. He wasn't sure if Sharyn was playing chicken or chess.

"Of course, I can only make a recommendation to the D.A."

"Of course."

"We can look the other way on the robbery *if* he has something strong enough that he can and will use to testify against the killer."

Percy smiled and Willy nodded his head.

"Hitting me in the eye is another story. The best I can do with that is probably eighteen months in county."

Willy shuddered and Percy turned back to Sharyn. "Since he hasn't *officially* been charged with that crime, and you do need his information, I think you could bend to thirty days in county and have him do some community service."

"Thirty days?" Sharyn balked. "I'm going to do a press conference tomorrow!"

Percy looked at Willy. "Ninety days and community service?"

She played with her removable pen cap. "Ninety days in county, two hundred hours community service. He cleans himself up and gets a job."

"What?" Willy stood up. "You can't make a man take a bath or get a job! That's unconstitutional!"

Percy grasped Willy's arm and pulled him down into his chair. He whispered into his ear again and Willy subsided, slumping back.

"Agreed," Percy said quickly. "Are you getting all of this, Dr. Thomopolis?"

"Sure," Nick replied without looking up.

"Okay," Sharyn responded. "Let's hear the information. If it works and he's willing to testify, I'll make my recommendation to the D.A. on his behalf."

Willy didn't look at her. "I saw the man come out of the motel. A little while before, I heard a woman crying. Those walls are thin. I heard arguing. The man comes out. He was tall, kind of thin. He was driving a dark car. I don't know what kind. It was big."

Sharyn waited. Willy didn't say anything else. "Is that it? Not even a partial license plate?"

Percy sat back in his chair. "It was more than you had before, Sheriff."

"Would you know the man if you saw him again, Willy? Could you pick him out of a lineup?"

"Sure. When he first came out of the room, the light was shining right in his face. I'd know him. He was wearing a hat so I don't know about his hair but I'd know his face."

"Could you help us draw a picture of him?"

He glanced at Percy who nodded. "I think so."

"Good. You've got a deal, Mr. Percy." Sharyn put out her hand to the attorney. He barely touched his cold fingers to hers.

"Nice doing business with you, Sheriff."

There was a knock on the door. David glanced in at them. "What's going on?"

"David, take Mr. Newsome back down to holding. We'll be filing charges against him for assault on a police officer," Sharyn explained.

David took a look at her eye and his face grew dark. "Come on. I can't believe you took a swing at the sheriff!"

JP watched as David took Willy past him. "Anything you need me to do, Sheriff?"

"No, this is it, JP, thanks. I'm going home for a few hours. How'd the domestic disturbance go?"

"They agreed to counseling. They were both in such bad shape, it was hard to tell who to arrest for abuse!"

"I'll be going, Sheriff," Percy told her. "My card if you need me again for this case."

"Mr. Percy," she said, taking his business card. "Just one thing."

"Yes, Sheriff?"

"Why did you do this for Willy? Everyone knows—"

"I was in Vietnam, Sheriff. There's not a vet in this town that doesn't have my business card. It's my little part of giving back to the community."

She nodded, surprised by his generosity. "Thanks, sir. We'll be in touch."

"Sharyn, you should have that looked at by a doctor," David told her when he came up from downstairs. He stood very close to her and smiled warmly into her face.

"I'm fine, David. Except for being exhausted. I'm going home for a shower and a few hours sleep. Call me if you need me."

"Yes, ma'am," JP answered smartly.

"Don't worry, Sharyn." David winked at her. "We'll take care of things."

Sharyn and Nick walked out together. The stars were bright beside a brilliant crescent moon that hung over Diamond Mountain.

"What was that all about?" Nick asked as he walked her to her Jeep.

"What?"

"David! Don't tell me you didn't notice him gazing deeply into your eyes and trying to look soulful? He winked at you!"

"I'm tired, Nick. I'm going home. I think you should do the same. Get some sleep. David is always strange. Send Ernie a copy of those notes tomorrow, huh?"

"Sure," he muttered. "And Sharyn?"

"Yes?"

He took her in his arms and kissed her sweetly on the side of her mouth. "Take *that* to bed with you! See you tomorrow."

SHARYN ARRIVED AT the office late. She'd overslept and her mother was walking around the house like a zombie. Ernie met her at the back door, as always.

"Heard you had some excitement here last night?"

"Don't ask," she replied, mindful of her eye.

Ernie considered the bruise around her eye. "Not too bad."

"That's because it's not your eye!"

"Grumpy this morning? Nick sent me the notes from the meeting you had with Eldeon Percy last night. He's a trip, isn't he?"

"You know him?"

"Sure. Every Vietnam vet in Diamond Springs knows him. I was glad you gave Willy a break, by the way."

"What happened to him, Ernie? How did he get to be that way? He was a hero."

"I don't know exactly. I just know that I've watched

it happen to a lot of good men. Heroes, I guess. I remember when Willy came home. We sat next to each other on the plane coming from San Francisco. He was full of plans and dreams just like the rest of us."

Sharyn shook her head. "Can we get Hubert to come up from the college to work with Willy on that sketch?"

"Already gave him a call. I've got notes from the group findings on the senator's car. Nick just sent them over." He looked at her strangely as she took off her gun and hat. "What was Nick doing here last night at midnight?"

"He came by to talk about what he'd found at the two crime scenes," she answered flatly. "I need a cup of coffee. Get everybody together, Ernie. When we have the sketch of the man Willy says he saw walk out of the motel, we're going to have to put together a serious effort to find him. Any info back from Nebraska?"

"A folder full of it. Nick says he heard back from Edith Randolph's doctor, too."

"Good. Let's get it all together then put Willy and Hubert together. I'd like to put this behind us."

He nodded and glanced at his clipboard full of notes. "I'll have someone drive out and pick Willy up."

"Pick him up? Did they transfer him to county during the night?"

"No." He looked at his notes again. "He was released on his own in early court this morning. About an hour ago."

"What?" Her mouth tightened and she winced. "Eldeon Percy convinced someone that Willy wasn't a flight risk?"

"He didn't handle it. His protégé was there for the bail hearing."

"And the D.A. thought it was all right to release Willy with no bail?"

"I guess so."

"Trudy!" Sharyn barked. "Get me Jack Winter on the line, please!"

"Yes, ma'am."

Sharyn sat down at her desk, drumming her fingers on the wood.

"Sheriff?" Jack Winter's smooth-as-silk voice came over the line. "What can I do for you?"

"Why did you advise no bail for Willy Newsome?"

"You were lenient with him. I thought I should be, too."

"You could have talked to me."

"*You* weren't in the office! I looked at the file. What seems to be the problem?"

"You let a man go who has no real permanent address, who attacked me and tried to get away last night, and who will probably take me all day to find!"

"Sharyn," he chided her. "You should have told

me it was so important to you. I would have taken care of it."

"Never mind," she replied. "I'll take care of it."

There was a click on the other end of the line. Sharyn looked at the receiver then replaced it in the cradle. "Let's find Willy. Have Joe and Ed run down to the motel. You and I will take the address he has listed."

Ernie nodded. "I would've called you, Sheriff, if I'd known this wasn't part of the deal."

"It doesn't matter," she decided with a deep breath. "Let's just find him and get him back here."

"He's always lived in Diamond Springs, if it's any consolation," Ernie told her. "I don't think he'll go anywhere."

"Let's hope not. He's probably our only chance of finding out who killed this woman."

"Sheriff, what do you want me to do?" Cari asked when Joe and Ed had been dispatched.

"Stay here and try to organize what we have on Edith Randolph. I don't want to have to wade through this woman's whole life if we can help it. I'm just looking for why she was here and who might have wanted to kill her."

Cari sighed. "When will I be allowed out in the field?"

"When you've completed your training."

"Yes, ma'am."

"This is important, too, Cari," Sharyn reminded her. "I know it's not exciting—"

"No, ma'am."

"But neither is this black eye, and I've had lots of training."

Cari sighed again. "Yes, ma'am."

Ernie picked up his gun and hat. He met Sharyn at the back door that led to the impound lot. "You didn't cuff him last night before you let him out, did you?"

Sharyn glanced at him. "You drive. I'll just sit over on the side and wallow in guilt."

Ernie laughed at her. "Anyone can make a mistake, Sheriff. Even *you!*"

"Sharyn." David approached them as they were getting into the squad car.

She was surprised to see him. "David? Why are you still out?"

"I was out looking for any last crime before I went home."

"Where's JP?" Ernie stifled a smile.

"I sent him home. He was tired." David swept his gaze out over the street next to the lot. "I wanted to be sure things were locked down before I went home."

Ernie rolled his eyes and asked for patience. "And? We're kind of in a hurry, David."

"I know. You're looking for Willy. I picked it up on the radio."

"Well?"

David took Sharyn's hand. "You don't have to worry about it, Sheriff."

She studied him for a moment, wondering if Nick was right. There was something strange about David. Of course, there was *always* something strange about David. "And?"

"He's dead. I called Joe and Ed to meet us there. I left a message for Nick. I found him near a Dumpster over on Meadowbrook by the playhouse."

Sharyn narrowed her eyes. "You didn't kill him, did you?"

"Of course not! Not when I knew how valuable he was to you. Would you like to ride over with me?"

She moved her hand from his. "Go home, David. You've done a good job, but I need you fresh for your shift."

"Okay." He grinned at her and winked again. "You're the sheriff."

Sharyn closed her car door as Ernie started the engine. "What's up with him?"

"I don't know." She shuddered.

"Don't tell me—"

"Don't even suggest it!"

"You and *David*?"

"No!"

Ernie swung the car out of the parking lot. "It make sense in a weird way."

"It isn't happening, Ernie," she protested.

"You *are* the same age. You've known each other practically your whole lives."

"He never even noticed me until I became sheriff and it made him mad."

Ernie grinned at her. "There's nothing wrong with it! You need someone in your life. Since Annie and I got together, it's like a whole new world."

"David and I aren't sharing a whole new world together," she rebuked. "Let's get back to the case, please?"

"No wonder you've been different. You were probably mooning over him last night and that's why you forgot to cuff Willy!" He laughed and patted her hand. "Don't worry. Your secret is safe. For now."

Sharyn ground her teeth and wished she could tell him the truth, but it was even stranger than David suddenly having a crush on her. At least, she felt like it was. She refused to think it was anything else but a crush. If David was thinking about her that way, he'd get over it quickly. He always did.

JOE AND ED were waiting for them at the Dumpster behind the playhouse. Willy was lying facedown in a puddle on the side of the huge Dumpster.

"What happened?" Sharyn asked.

"Two shots. One to the head. One to the chest.

Looks like they shot him in the chest first then came up close to finish the job," Joe said.

"Have you had a chance to look around?"

"No, not yet," Ed replied. "We just got here."

She looked down the alleyway. The playhouse was the only building there. Behind them was an empty lot full of scrub trees where the city had pulled down an old apartment complex. The dirty street was badly paved and full of debris.

Nick's car pulled up with the paramedic unit behind him. "David said Willy had been killed."

"Yeah," Ernie agreed. "Looks that way."

"Poor old guy." Joe shook his head. "With all the stuff he was into, it's no wonder someone finally did it."

"But did they have to do it *now?*" Sharyn demanded.

"Looks like he's got one of the prescription bottles in his hand," Nick observed, pulling on his gloves and crouching close to the body.

"Probably trying to sell it and get out of town," Ed theorized. "I don't know if he really could identify that man at the motel or not, Sheriff."

Sharyn shook her head. "It looks like we'll never know now."

"I'll take a look at him," Nick said. "But I doubt if there's going to be much on the body. This bottle is still full. These wounds weren't made close up.

JOYCE & JIM LAVENE 119

Chances are the killer didn't come near enough to leave anything behind."

"Yeah," Ernie continued. "And there's enough footprints and tire marks back here that you'd have to bring in half the county for questioning!"

"Do the best you can," Sharyn told Nick. "When you've got something, let me know. I want to get everyone together. We've got a lot of information and no answers."

"Sure thing," he remarked. "And Sheriff? Next time, remember to hold your right up and come back with your left."

Sharyn grimaced and followed Ernie back to the car as she spoke to Ed and Joe. "You guys, canvas the scene. See if you can find the weapon. See if anybody heard anything or saw anything. I'm sure Nick should have time of death for you in just a few seconds, as sharp as he is today!"

"There won't be much to go on," Ernie said as they got back in the squad car. "The playhouse was empty. There hasn't been a play there in a month. No one lives nearby."

"I know."

Ernie shook his head. "Two shootings, unrelated, and a woman dying from cancer smothered in her bed. And all in a few days. That must be a record for Diamond Springs."

"If I didn't know better," Sharyn answered, "I'd

think Jack Winter set it up to make me look bad. But even he has his limits."

"But he *did* let Willy go."

"Are you saying they were doing business together?"

Ernie shrugged. "Nope. And if he was, we'd never know about it."

"That's optimistic!"

"Where to?"

"Let's check out Willy's place," she decided. "Then we'll head back to the office and sort through this mess."

Willy's address turned out to be the basement of another Vietnam vet, Fred Sandler, who let him use it rent-free. There was an outer door to the basement, so Fred was never sure whether Willy was home or not. He wasn't much help beyond opening the door and letting them in.

"He was careful not to be associated with Willy, wasn't he?" Sharyn asked Ernie as they wandered through the basement.

"Would you want to be associated with Willy?" Ernie put on some latex gloves. "I know Fred. He's a decent guy with a wife and a family who probably hates Willy living here."

"But he let him stay. Did you know he lived here?"

"No, but it doesn't surprise me. There's a bond between all of us who were there, Sheriff. I can't explain it. We may not like each other or approve of each other but we're there for one another."

Sharyn continued looking through Willy's pitiful belongings. He slept on a pallet on the floor. There were a few pairs of jeans scattered around the room. A model aircraft and some pictures rested on the window ledge. The pictures were of Willy in his uniform.

"I think I may have found something here, Sheriff," Ernie told her. He picked up a ladies' handbag and gingerly searched the interior. "Yep. We got a winner. Edith Randolph's driver's license."

Sharyn looked at the wallet. There were pictures of a young boy all the way up to about age twelve. The discovery made her think again about Edith's worried family in Nebraska. She could have a husband and children who were frantically looking for her.

"I don't like this, Ernie."

"No, ma'am."

"It doesn't make any sense."

"I hate it when you say that."

"Let's get back to the office. We know Edith Randolph wasn't killed here. Whatever else went on here, I don't want to know. I don't think we're going to find anything about Willy's death besides his sad existence."

"I'm with you," Ernie told her with a deep indrawn breath. "This place makes me want to curl up in a ball and cry."

Sharyn put her hand on his shoulder, seeing his anguish for Willy. "Let's go."

THERE WERE GRIM faces at the sheriff's office later that afternoon. JP and David came in early. Trudy was holding all nonemergency calls. They clustered around the big conference table, while Nick and Ernie distributed information to them.

David had immediately taken a chair beside Sharyn, sitting a little closer than necessary. Nick frowned from the other side of the table, but kept his word on his deal with Sharyn.

"Well, we appear to be in the middle of Diamond Springs' first crime wave," Nick said as he finished passing out photocopies. "Where do you want to start?"

"Let's start at the beginning," Sharyn decided. "What about Senator Talbot's shooting?"

"I haven't heard back about the muskets yet," Nick told her. "The car is another matter. The preliminary findings were gravel from the parking lot at the old mill along with cornmeal on the driver's side. The car is full of prints that belong to the senator and his aid, Sloane Philips, which is what we would expect to find since they both drive the car. There were a few prints from Faye Howard on the steering wheel but again, not totally unexpected and probably not related to the case."

"Is that it?" Joe asked him.

Nick shrugged. "My conclusion is that whoever shot the senator drove his car away because he was hoping no one would know he was there. He found a side road and ditched it in the trees behind a field of hay. He banged it up, maybe hoping that whoever found it wouldn't think it was the same car."

"Footprints, tire tracks?" Ernie suggested.

"We had violent thunderstorms the night of the shooting, and more since then. The hay was cut down after the car was put there. There's zip. Oh, except for another interesting set of prints from Kristie Howard and Keith Reynolds along with a few other *items* in the backseat."

"I don't think that's pertinent to the case," Sharyn said without looking up. "Can we move on?"

"That's it. The senator can't or won't cooperate. The evidence at the mill is too general because of the traffic. The only thing left would be to link the musket to the man who owns it," Ed concluded.

"And that probably wouldn't amount to anything," Joe finished for him.

Sharyn nodded. "Let's move on. Edith Randolph."

"Everything points to Willy having killed her, except that those aren't his handprints on the top of the pillowcase," Nick said.

"Maybe he changed the pillowcase," Cari added. Everyone looked at her and she shrugged.

"I really think this was the pillowcase and the pillow she was smothered with," Nick told her.

"Could Willy have washed his hands, and while he was pressing down, it made his hands look bigger?" JP suggested.

"I don't think that's possible. Willy had very small hands. I checked again one last time while I was examining him. These hands belong to a bigger man. And a cleaner man."

"Okay, but doesn't it impress anyone else that Willy said he could ID the man who killed the woman, and now he's dead, too?" Cari glanced around the table at them.

"That fact impresses *me*," Sharyn agreed with her. "I'll let you follow that idea, Cari. See what you can come up with. What about Edith herself?"

Cari passed out sheets of paper to everyone. "I checked out everything I could about Edith Randolph. She moved to Chadron, Nebraska, about seven years ago. She was very quiet. Her neighbors didn't know her well. In fact, they didn't even know she had cancer. She sold her house about three weeks ago. It was a fast sale. They didn't know where she was going or what she was doing. She just left."

"Dr. Nym Paddah, the oncologist who was treating Ms. Randolph for advanced pancreatic cancer, said she wasn't very forthcoming about herself. She was fifty-seven years old. She was unmarried. If she had a son, Dr. Paddah never met him while she was undergoing treatment. He said her records didn't show her having any children." Nick put down his glasses. "The woman was a mystery."

"But how did she end up here?" Ernie asked.

"Dr. Paddah's theory is that when people know they're going to die, they do strange things. He said he told Edith about three weeks ago that she had less than a month to live, and suspended treatment at her request. He said it's not unheard of for a person without family to take off and go somewhere to die."

"What about Mr. Martin's claim that she came in on a bus?" Sharyn asked.

"There's no record of anyone named Edith Randolph or Eleanor Roosevelt being on a bus in or out of Diamond Springs in the last two months," Ed told her. "At least not using a credit card. That's as far as the bus line will go."

"So, we come back to the man in the dark car," JP summed up.

"Exactly," Sharyn agreed. "Let's look at what we have. The man in the dark car wasn't someone Willy knew, yet it was someone he believed he would recognize again if he saw him."

"*If* he was telling the truth and not just saying that to beat a robbery rap," Nick reminded her.

"Okay." Sharyn glared at him. "*If* he was telling the truth."

"How many large, dark cars can there be in Diamond Springs?" Cari wondered. "We could check with DMV."

"That might work," Sharyn supported her. "But the list would be pretty long. I think I saw about twenty on the street this morning. Let's assume that it was someone from Diamond Springs who killed her, not someone who followed her from Nebraska. This woman doesn't seem to be the kind of person who would have an assassin following her. Ernie, let's find out if the boy in these wallet pictures is her son. Maybe she was here to see him."

David added his first remark. "Maybe they argued about her money and he killed her."

"Why bother?" Ed debated. "He only had to wait a few days for her to die."

"We have her canceled bank-account statement," Cari told him. "She never had more than a weekly paycheck in her account."

He sighed. "Well, I guess we'll find out."

Everyone was surprised that he didn't argue with the pair after weeks of feuding with them ever since Ed started dating Cari, but no one said anything. It was too good to last.

"Okay, let's see if we can crack this thing. I feel like I left my laundry out in the rain and I can't get it dry," Sharyn told them. "I'm doing an interview and a rally later today, so coordinate with Ernie. Call me if anyone finds out anything."

David stood up and smiled at her. "Don't worry, Sharyn. We'll find out the truth. We all want you to win the election."

"What's the matter with him?" Nick asked Ed aside from the group.

Ed folded his papers together. "David told me that he forgave me because something better has happened for him."

Cari crowded close. "I think he means him and the sheriff! I think they might be secretly dating."

Nick wanted to laugh. He really did. After all the innuendoes and outright gossip about him and Sharyn for almost a year, they were pairing her up with David. But only after he and Sharyn had discovered that there was something *to* the innuendoes and gossip.

"Sorry, old son." Ernie tried to comfort him as they walked out of the conference room together. "You just waited too long. She's a young woman. She was bound to be thinking about having a man in her life once she got over her daddy's death."

Nick *wanted* to laugh. He also wanted to crack the tabletop with his fist. But he'd promised Sharyn he'd be patient. And in the middle of everything that was going on, now wasn't a good time to press the issue.

What did he care if everyone thought she was dating David? He knew she was dating *him*.

Or *would* be when there was time.

SIX

SHARYN WAS BACK from the rally and the interview with Foster Odom by six o'clock. Ernie was just leaving, but he stayed a few minutes to brief her on what they'd found while she was gone.

"I won't tell you how many large, dark cars Cari found listed in Montgomery County."

"Thanks." She looked at the twenty or so names on the list. "What about Edith's son?"

"If he lives in Diamond Springs, he has a different name."

"Or she may have changed hers," Sharyn suggested, opening her mail. "Maybe the Nebraska DMV has a listing for her under another name. She *was* wearing a wedding band...the son might have the father's name."

Ernie lips twitched. "I'll fax them before I leave. How did the interview and rally go?"

"The rally was fine. The interview was just Foster Odom trying to make me look bad. I'm sure by the time he gets done with it, I will."

"You sound tired," he remarked.

"I am, but only because I slept about three hours last night. I'll be fine."

"Hear anything from Kristie?"

"She called once. She says she's fine and enjoying staying with Aunt Selma. I wanted to go out and see her, but Aunt Selma said no. She says Kristie is beating herself up because she's not as strong as I am."

"She'll get over it," Ernie promised. "She's as tough a Howard as any of you. She'll pull through."

"I think Mom will be better now that the senator is at home. You know how she feels about hospitals."

"I know. She had to stand outside and wave to your daddy that one time he was shot. If it wasn't so pitiful, it would've been funny."

Sharyn smiled. "I'll be okay, Ernie. Go home to Annie. Remember, we only get to keep you if I don't make you stay late all the time. I'm going to go through this mail and go home, too."

Ernie smiled. "About this thing with you and David—"

"Please, Ernie, not tonight."

"Okay. But I like it. You need someone you can lean on besides the people you work with. Everyone does. For a long time, I thought it might be—"

She shook her head. "I just can't talk about it yet."

He made a face at her. "I'm not going anywhere. Night, Sheriff."

"Good night, Ernie."

"Sheriff, can I get you a cup of coffee or anything before we go out on patrol?" David wanted to know.

"No, thanks, David. Are you and JP checking out that drug bust out on the interstate?"

"Yeah. Ernie told us to coordinate with the high-way patrol. I would have taken care of the whole thing but he wouldn't let me."

"What you have is enough, David. Have a good night."

"Will you be here when we get back?"

"I hope not."

"Poor little thing," he commiserated, moving close to her. "You look exhausted."

"David!" She was ready to tell him to back off, but then he smiled sweetly at her and she sighed. "Thanks. I'll be fine."

Everyone had said their good-nights. JP and David were out on patrol. Sharyn had finished her mail, but was too tired to get up and go home. If her mother was there, she would have to deal with her torrents of tears. If she wasn't there, the house just seemed strangely empty. She was beginning to understand why her father had such a comfortable chair in his office.

But she was too restless to sit in one place with her feet up. The box containing Edith Randolph's property was on the floor beside her desk. She got down on the floor next to it and began to sift through the contents.

It was hard for Sharyn to believe that the woman had owned a whole house and that this box was all she'd brought out of it. Of course, she'd known she was dying. Maybe it didn't make sense to keep anything else. She looked at Edith's wedding band. It was plain yellow gold, no inscription. Her other ring was a single stone that looked like a sapphire.

A clap of thunder shook the office. Sharyn jumped and saw that Marvella had come in to clean.

"Looks like we're gonna have another thunderstorm tonight! Too much noise and not enough rain! What are you doing down there, Sheriff?"

"Looking through what's left of a woman's life."

Marvella shook her feather duster. "There'll be more than that when I go!"

Sharyn smiled at her. "I'm sure there was more than this that Edith owned, too. She just chose to give it all up and travel light, I guess."

"You looked good at that rally today, Sheriff," Marvella complimented. "But stop wearing that uniform when you go to those political things. Puts ten pounds on you! Nobody else was wearing a uniform."

"No one else is the sheriff, but thanks." Sharyn digested the information.

Marvella went on and Sharyn looked through the contents of Edith's wallet. There was no money, no credit cards. Just her driver's license and those pictures of a boy who might or might not be her son. They were checking the hospitals in Nebraska again for her son's possible birth. She hated to think that Edith had a son somewhere who didn't know that his mother was dead. On the other hand, why hadn't she told her doctor that she had a child when she was dying?

She picked up the tiny gold locket that was wrapped in plastic. It looked as though it could open. She knew Nick was done with it, so she slipped on gloves and opened up the package.

It was stubborn. Sharyn finally got her letter opener to pry open the locket face. Inside were two very small pictures. They were very grainy, and shot in black and white. They looked like reduced versions from one of those photo machines. One was a man, and one was a woman.

Sharyn was barely able to make out Edith's features in the picture when she held her magnifying glass over it. She was much younger, much prettier. Her hair looked blond in the photo but it was impossible to tell for sure. Sharyn pried out the picture with her fingernail and looked at the back. *E.T.*

She smiled as 'extraterrestrial' passed her mind. Maybe Edith's married name started with a *T.* Or maybe her maiden name? She looked at the picture of the man. Was this her absent husband? Father?

Brother? Under the magnifying glass there was something vaguely familiar about the man in the photo. She couldn't quite place what it was. It gnawed at the back of her mind but nothing substantial came from it. She pried the tiny picture out of the locket and looked at the back. There was something there, but it had been scratched out.

She looked at the pictures in her hands for a long time. Finally, she closed her eyes and decided to go home. It wasn't doing any good sitting there looking at Edith Randolph's possessions. Maybe if she were a psychic, she could look at them and gain some knowledge about the dead woman. As it was, her eyes were crossing with the effort. She picked everything up and put it back into the box.

"Going home now, Sheriff?" Marvella asked without turning around from cleaning a computer screen.

"Yes. Good night, Marvella."

"Wear something floaty. Maybe chiffon," the cleaning lady advised. "It would soften your look."

"I'd like to, but I'm not trying to run a dance school," Sharyn answered. "The uniform will have to do."

"All right." Marvella smiled and looked at her. "Don't worry. Like I said, it doesn't really matter what you wear. You're gonna win this election."

"Thanks. See you later, Marvella."

The house was dark when Sharyn got home. She

guessed Faye was with the senator. Bone-tired from the events of the last few days, Sharyn let herself into the house. She opened and closed the refrigerator door but didn't have the energy to eat anything. The house smelled like her mother's perfume.

Her mother had offered to let her have the house to live in after she and Caison were married, but Sharyn didn't think that was going to work. There were too many memories of living here as a family with her parents and Kristie. When the time came, she was going to have to look for a place of her own. She dreaded it, but it was the only answer.

She went and sat in her father's den. Nothing much had changed in there since he'd died. Sharyn and Kristie had given him the big, comfortable La-Z-Boy chair he'd loved so much. His desk was clean. When he was alive, it was always cluttered.

The room still felt like him. It reminded her how much she missed him. It was a comfortable place to be, unlike her mother's formal living room where the lime-green and lemon-yellow furniture was covered in plastic. She never sat in there when she could help it.

Restless still, despite being tired, she went and sat at his desk. She looked at the pictures of herself and Kristie as children. She picked up her father's badge and dusted it off. The pens that he picked up everywhere he went were still there, as well as the read-

ing glasses from the drugstore because he refused
to go and buy real glasses from a doctor. There were
matchbooks from restaurants around the area, and
mint-flavored toothpicks covered in plastic.

Looking at his things was like looking at the box
that belonged to Edith Randolph. Except that there
was a bittersweet pang that clutched at her heart when
she thought about her father. She'd been lucky to have
him, to be close to him for so long. But losing him
had changed her life forever. She felt like she'd become an adult that day.

Sharyn closed the drawer and stood up. She looked
at the collection of pictures on the wall. Most of them
were pictures with friends. Many of them were pictures with Ernie, Joe and Ed at work. There was one
with her grandfather on the day T. Raymond had become sheriff. He was shaking his father's hand.

Another picture caught her attention. She'd looked
at it so many times that it was as familiar as her own
face. It was a picture of her father and Caison Talbot
in a boat. They were fishing down by the dam on the
Pee Dee River. It was taken long before Caison was
senator, before her father was sheriff. It was just two
friends out for the day. The smiles on their faces and
the way they sat together for the picture told its own
story about how close they were at that time.

Sharyn wondered who the third person was taking
that picture. She glanced at it once more, then stopped

short. With trembling fingers, she picked up her father's glasses and looked through them at the picture. The man sitting beside her father was the same man in the picture that was lodged in Edith Randolph's locket. *Caison Talbot.*

Suddenly, too many of the puzzle pieces fell into place. She snatched up the picture and ran out of the house.

THE THUNDERSTORM HAD become progressively worse as the night wore on. Rain slashed against the window, and lightning illuminated the sky. Thunder was booming so loudly and regularly that Nick thought it sounded like someone knocking on his door. Then he realized that it *was* someone knocking on his door. The pounding went on until he finally got up and threw on his robe. He stalked to the front door and swung it open wide.

"Do you have any idea what time it is?" he demanded.

Sharyn glanced at her watch. "Almost three."

Nick stared at her. She was standing in the hallway dripping water, still in her uniform. "Are you still working?"

"Can I come in?"

"Yeah. Sure." He ran his hand through his hair and across the dark beard on his chin. "I'm not exactly ready for company."

"Don't think of me as company," she admonished, following him into his apartment. "I'm the sheriff."

"Okay, Sheriff. Want some coffee?" He yawned and wandered into the kitchen.

"Nick, I've just realized something."

"You couldn't wake Ernie up?"

"Well, that too," she admitted. Ernie was a notoriously deep sleeper.

"This doesn't count as our second date."

"Nick!"

He sat down at the glass kitchen table and gestured for her to do the same. "What now?"

She'd already gone by the office and picked up Edith's locket. She put the pictures from it beside the picture of her father and Caison on the table. "Look at this."

"Just a minute." He stopped her. "Let me get my glasses."

Sharyn had made two cups of coffee by the time he returned with his glasses. He'd changed into slacks and a T-shirt and combed his hair. He took a moment to brush his teeth. He didn't know why she was there, but—

He sat down again and smiled at the coffee.

"Two sugars, black, right?" She grinned at him.

"Right." He put on his glasses and looked at the two pictures. "Where did you get this?"

"The small one is from Edith Randolph's locket."

He examined the smaller picture first. Then he looked at the larger picture. "This is T. Raymond, isn't it?"

"Yes. The man beside him is Caison Talbot."

"No!" Nick looked at the pictures again. There was no doubting that both pictures were of the same man. He looked up at Sharyn's unhappy face. "You're kidding me? Edith Randolph was here to look for Senator Talbot?"

"I don't know that yet," she said, getting up and pacing the floor. "But his picture is in a locket that she was wearing. Her initials on the back of her picture in the locket are E.T."

"Like the movie?"

"Only scarier."

Nick took off his glasses and rubbed his eyes. "I don't even want to think how this is going to go down."

"Nick, it all makes a terrible logic. The tall, thin man outside of Edith's room that night. The big, dark car."

"Are you suggesting that the senator killed Edith?"

"I don't know what I'm suggesting yet." She shrugged and continued pacing. "I think when I can get Ernie up, we're going to have to go and see the senator and try to make some sense out of it. I don't want to say anything or do anything until I know what's going on."

"And you think he's going to tell you? He wouldn't even tell you who shot him!"

Sharyn frowned. "That's the part I don't get. Caison smothers this woman, who may or may not have been his wife. Then the next morning, he gets up early and goes out to the old mill by himself and someone shoots him? That's a lot of action even for the senator."

"Maybe the two events *are* related," he suggested, still looking at the pictures.

"How?"

"I don't know. Maybe Willy was more involved than you thought. Maybe he was involved with Edith Randolph and he tried to take the senator out because he knew Caison killed Edith. He shot the senator but Caison knew who he was and he followed up and shot Willy behind the theater."

Sharyn stared at him. "I can't believe the senator would be so careless. Or for that matter, that he would do any of his own dirty work."

"Some things you can't trust to hired help. If the senator and Willy were both personally involved with Edith, it could explain him taking those chances."

"I still can't believe it."

Nick stood beside her. "Sharyn, you're running on low fuel right now."

"What do you mean?"

"Look at yourself. You're vibrating with caffeine,

you probably haven't eaten in ten or twelve hours, and you haven't slept. You don't want to take on the senator like this."

She put her hands on his arms. "Nick, if I'm wrong about this, it would cost him his career. My mother will never speak to me again. Jack Winter's job offer is starting to look better and better."

"Don't even joke about a thing like that," he warned gruffly. "Let me put some shoes on and we'll both go pound on Ernie's door. We'll work through the whole thing and make sure it all fits together before you confront Senator Talbot."

"I don't want to drag you out into the streets, Nick," she replied. "I just needed someone else to look at this picture besides Marvella!"

"Marvella? Did you show it to Marvella before you came here?"

"Of course not! But she was the only one available at the office. David and JP were out on the interstate with the highway patrol, handling a drug bust."

He shook his head. "Let me get my shoes."

When he came back, he looked at her standing by the window that overlooked Diamond Mountain Lake. He walked up behind her and put his hands on her shoulders. "How's your eye?"

"Much better." She touched it lightly. "Willy didn't swing much of a punch."

"Thank goodness," he said, then touched his mouth to hers quickly. "I'm ready to go when you are."

Sharyn walked out before him. Nick was switching off his lights when he said, "About David—"

She groaned. "Not now, Nick. You know him. He'll be over it in a day or two."

"If I don't kill him first," he muttered, closing the door hard behind him.

By 4:00 A.M., the storm had abated, leaving Diamond Springs' streets shiny black and covered with debris from the battered oaks that stood guard around them. The wind from the mountains still howled, and the distant rumble of thunder still echoed, but the worst of the storm had passed.

Ernie, Nick, Ed and Sharyn sat huddled around a cheap Formica table at the local diner. They each nursed a cup of coffee. Ed had a few donuts. The diner was empty except for the waitress who dozed in the corner, and the cook who was making grits for the morning rush.

The pictures Sharyn had found were between them on the table. They had each looked at them and come up with the same conclusion.

"Of course the pictures are both grainy, and the locket picture is distorted," Ernie said into the silence.

"We could have a lab clean that up in a few hours," Nick replied.

"It wouldn't be conclusive proof of anything," Ed offered with a yawn. "Even if it *is* Senator Talbot, without Willy you can't prove he was at the motel."

"That's true," Ernie echoed. "Any more than you could prove that Willy shot the senator. The only thing in your favor on that is that Willy probably could've figured out how to use the musket if he was sober that day."

"There's an easy way to prove or disprove the senator's guilt," Nick concluded. "We match a print of his palms with the palm prints on the pillow used to smothered Edith Randolph. Either his hands fit, or they don't. I even have a lead on the soap the killer washed his hands with before the event. I'm just waiting for the lab report to come back."

"What about Willy?" Sharyn asked.

"He was shot with a .45 Firestorm. Nice gun. Something someone might have for protection. If we had a gun, we could match up the slugs. One shot would have killed him. I guess the killer didn't want to take any chances."

"Wouldn't it surprise you if the senator *doesn't* carry a gun, even with all his protection?" Ed reasoned with a wicked smile.

"Don't get too arrogant about this, Ed," Sharyn warned. "This will be hard to prove, and even more disastrous if we do prove it."

"Especially for you," Ernie said with a grim smile

at her. "Your mama might take it a little personally if you put her fiancé in prison."

"Not to mention the fact that everyone knows how you feel about Talbot, Sheriff," Ed reminded her. "How are you gonna do this without everyone and their brothers saying you helped it along?"

"Proof," she answered clearly. "Conclusive proof. Unless the senator wants to confess."

"Yeah, that's gonna happen." Ernie yawned. "What do you need from me?"

"Let's focus on how Edith Randolph and Caison Talbot could have known each other. And what his motive would be to kill her."

"Okay."

"And let's keep this quiet. I don't want the press sniffing around this until we know for sure. If he's guilty of something, fine. If not, I don't want to ruin Senator Talbot's career."

Ed yawned. "If you don't need me specifically, I'm going home to try and straighten all of this out with Cari."

"What happened?" Ernie asked.

"She thought I was flirting with the waitress at supper last night."

They all groaned.

"What?" Ed demanded. "I wasn't flirting! The girl was coming on to me!"

"Oh, Ed, we all know better. Get your behind over

there and apologize to that nice little girl!" Ernie shook his head and finished his coffee. "I can stay, Sheriff. Annie is going to sit with her mother anyway. They called from the nursing home again. Mary Sue is having nightmares and these storms aren't helping."

"All the years she lived with Delbert, not knowing what really happened," Sharyn considered. She looked up at Ernie. "I don't want my mother to go through that with Caison. We have to get to the truth."

"And make ourselves look good by catching the killer, then make ourselves look bad because the killer is our senator!" Ed finished his donut. "I'm going to see Cari. But I'll come in as soon as I'm done."

"Thanks, Ed," Sharyn acknowledged.

"It's the least I can do since ya'll were nice enough to meet me here. I thought I was just coming out for some donuts and coffee! I couldn't believe it when I saw you sitting here."

Nick nodded. "And they say New York never sleeps!"

"Neither does Diamond Springs," Ernie returned.

"Or at least her sheriff," Nick added.

"Thanks, guys," Sharyn said, getting to her feet. "See you later, Ed."

"I'm going to go back to my office," Nick said to her. "Maybe I can lean on my friend a little and get those muskets done faster. Plus I still have some paperwork to process on Willy."

"Thanks, Nick." She smiled at him slowly. "For everything."

"No problem, Sheriff."

Ernie shook his head as they walked across the street together to the sheriff's office. A watery dawn was easing up over the peaks of the Uwharrie Mountains. Diamond Springs was beginning to wake up, but the usually bustling streets were still empty.

"I'm on the fence with this one, Sheriff," he admitted.

"I know, Ernie. Me, too." She shivered in the damp morning chill.

"I don't want it to be the senator."

"Neither do I."

"I believe you. I just wonder how many other people will."

She glanced at him. "Are you saying you think I should excuse myself from this case if we find out Caison is involved?"

He stopped and looked her in the eye. "Sheriff, you should probably excuse yourself right now since we *think* it could be the senator. I know some people who might believe *you* shot him at the old mill! It's no secret that the two of you don't get along."

Sharyn considered his words. "You're right."

"But you're not gonna do it, are you?"

"No, probably not."

"You're stubborn like your daddy."

"I know. But where would we be if I'd taken Michaelson's advice and excused myself from *your* investigation?"

"You have a good point, ma'am."

David and JP were still out. The office was empty when they got there.

"So, where do we start?"

"Let's go over the senator's shooting."

Ernie got out his notes.

"What time did his aide say he saw the senator last?"

"'About 6:00 p.m. on Saturday. Phillips parked the Lincoln in the garage after he dropped the senator off at the house. The senator had been preoccupied for days,'" he read aloud from the text. "We know he drove himself to the mill the next morning. He didn't say anything to anyone, so your mama and Sloane Phillips thought he was missing."

"He told me that he wanted to be alone at the mill when I went to see him," Sharyn said.

"But how does his shooting play into Edith Randolph's murder? Why would the senator kill her when she was already dying? He's not stupid, Sheriff. He could've waited her out like a spider waiting for a fly."

"Maybe he didn't have time." She shrugged. "Maybe she had something on him that she threatened to expose. Maybe that's why she was here. His acting preoccupied does fit in well with her arrival."

"And Willy? What's the theory here? That Willy tried to kill Caison because he knew Caison had killed Edith Randolph. Then Caison killed Willy because he shot him?"

"I don't know, Ernie." She rested her head in her hands. "Maybe Willy knew what Edith had on Caison and he threatened to use it against him?"

"Then why try to kill Caison?"

"Maybe he tried to blackmail him first and that didn't work. We all thought the senator's shooting wasn't planned. Maybe Willy *wasn't* involved with Edith beyond seeing the senator there that night. Maybe he tried to get money from the senator to keep his mouth shut."

"Sounds like a lot of activity for Willy, Sheriff." Ernie scratched his head. "If he made it to the streetlight and back each day, he was doing well."

"Maybe. But it would have been a big score for Willy. Maybe one that would've lasted the rest of his life if he could've pulled it off. If we're right, there's a link between Edith and the senator. We just have to find it."

"So this woman knew something bad about the senator, and when she found out she was dying, she wanted to come here and hurt him?" He looked at Sharyn. "How likely is that?"

"I know it doesn't make any sense. We're missing some piece of the puzzle."

"Wish I could help," Ernie said, handing her a fax. "But it looks like Edith Randolph has always used her name, according to the DMV. Here's a photocopy of her driver's license record. Clean as a whistle and always Edith Randolph."

"The neighbors said she moved to her house about seven years ago," Sharyn pointed out. "I wonder where she lived before that?"

"Wherever it was, she kept her Nebraska driver's license," he replied. "There's no break between the first license issued when she was eighteen and the last a few years ago. Different addresses on each one. She moved around a lot. But she always stayed in Nebraska."

"Until she came to North Carolina to die."

He nodded.

Sharyn shook her head. "I'm going to catch a quick shower, Ernie. Things will look better with a change of clothes."

He laughed. "You expect a lot from a shower and some clean clothes, Sheriff!"

"Yeah. I'll be back as soon as I can."

"I'm going to fax a query to the Nebraska police about her previous address. Maybe something will turn up there."

"Thanks, Ernie. Sorry to drag you out of bed then leave you here alone."

"Not alone." Ernie nodded towards the back door

where JP and David were wearily coming in for the night.

"Sheriff." JP smiled at her then looked at Ernie. "You're in early."

"It's been a long night," she told him.

"You should have called, Sharyn." David stepped closer to her. "I would've come and helped you."

"David, I think you had your hands full. How'd it go?"

"The state police got two guys. They're pretty broken up but they were transporting some marijuana and some cold pills."

"Cold pills?" Ernie asked.

"Yep. About twenty cases of cold medicine."

"They denied that they were selling them," JP explained. "They said they just had bad colds!"

"Both of you did a good job, thanks," Sharyn said, excusing herself.

"Sharyn?" David called to her as she was leaving.

"Yes?"

"I'd like to take you out for dinner some night. I don't come in until late, and you leave late. It could work out."

Sharyn had reached her breaking point with David's attention. "I don't think that's a good idea, David."

"Why? We like each other. We're adults."

"We're too different. And I'm the sheriff. I don't think it would look right for us to go out together."

"You're right." He winked at her and glanced back at Ernie and JP. "We'll have to sneak out together. No one can know."

She sighed. "I'll talk to you later, David."

"In private?"

"Yes."

On her way home, Sharyn refused to think about David's advances. They would end. David could hardly stay interested in one woman for more than a few hours. His interest in her would fade quickly, especially if she kept turning him down.

It struck her tired brain that she was moving backwards. She should have been leaving for work, and instead she was going home. She swung her Jeep into the drive and parked it. When she put her key in the lock on the door, she discovered it was already open.

Without another thought, Sharyn took out her gun and kept her back to the kitchen wall as she entered the house. Her heart was beating fast, adrenaline rushing through her system. She was glad her mother and Kristie were both away. At least she didn't have to worry about their safety.

She followed the wall into the green-and-yellow living room but it was empty. She went quickly through the dining room but there was no one there, either. She heard a sound from the direction of her father's den and followed it. Inching around the door, she pushed her gun into the room before her.

"Sharyn!" Jack Winter greeted her. "What a surprise. I thought you'd already left for work."

"I've been at work all night," she replied steadily, not putting the gun down. "What are you doing here? How did you get in?"

He put up his hands and held out a key to her. It was on her mother's key ring.

Sharyn lowered her gun and faced him. "What are you doing here?"

"I was looking for some papers that your father had been keeping for me. I asked Faye if I could come over. She was busy, so she gave me the key."

She snatched the key ring from his hand. "If you tell me what you need, I'll take a look around for you."

He smiled. "Thanks. That would save me some time and trouble."

"What kind of papers are they?"

"Oh, just notes from cases we'd worked on together. Nothing particularly interesting, but I'm thinking about writing my memoirs. I thought they'd help me."

"I'll be sure to check for them."

He studied her face. "You look tired. You shouldn't work so hard."

"Thanks for the advice."

"You don't trust me, do you?"

"No, sir. I don't."

"Your father trusted me. We worked on many cases together."

"I'm sure you did."

"How are those murder cases coming?"

"We're making progress," she answered blankly.

"Good. And the senator's shooting?"

"We're making progress on that, too."

"Fine. You'll let me know when you're ready to move on something?"

"Of course. You're the D.A."

He flashed her a smile that made her skin crawl. "We'd make a brilliant pair, you and I. I wish you'd rethink your distrust of me."

"I'm sure someday I will, Mr. Winter."

A car horn sounded from outside. "There's my ride. I'll talk with you later, Sharyn."

She didn't reply, but she watched him get in the limousine and saw it drive away. She didn't move from the window until she was sure that he was gone. Then she called to have all the locks in the house changed.

SEVEN

IT WAS ALL Sharyn could do to make herself stay in the house long enough to take a shower and get dressed. The awful feeling that Jack Winter had been there, possibly going through her personal belongings, lingered. How could her father have had any dealings with that man, except when absolutely necessary? Yet the casual way her mother gave him her keys told her that they were on familiar terms.

She called her mother from her cell phone and told her that there would be new locks on the doors. Faye was confused but went along with the change. She told Sharyn that Caison was feeling much stronger.

"Your mother makes a fine nurse," the senator said in the background.

A strong feeling of foreboding overcame her. The implications of Caison Talbot being involved in Edith Randolph's death were unnerving. She knew the "good old boy" system was working every day in Diamond Springs. She just didn't know to what extent, and she was terrified to find out. What if it involved her father? She came close enough to feel the hot breath of fear when she'd investigated her first murder as sheriff. There had been too many unanswered questions about her father, Caison Talbot, and George Albert, the ex-councilman. She hated that she'd been afraid to ask them.

"Just please don't give your keys to Mr. Winter again, Mom."

"Whyever not? He was a good friend of your father's."

"Trust me on this."

"All right, Sharyn. But I do believe you're being paranoid."

"Thanks. I'll get a key to you this afternoon, Mom." Her cell phone rang as she was about to put it down.

"Sheriff, we got a call from a man who says he's got some information about Willy's death," Trudy explained. "Ernie's on his way there now."

"Where?"

"Main and Magnolia. The old Clements building."

Sharyn did a fast mental geography. "That building's been empty for ten years."

"They tend to empty out fast once they burn up," Trudy answered with a laugh. "That's the address the man gave him. I think he might be an old friend of Ernie's."

"Thanks, Trudy."

Sharyn parked her Jeep in the street beside the old building and looked for Ernie's squad car. It was in the back. There had been a huge explosion and fire in the Clements Building when she was a teenager. The insurance company was still investigating and had protested loudly when the city had been about to tear the old hulk down. Seven people had died in that fire.

"Ernie?" she called out into the charred shell.

"Back here, Sheriff," he answered.

Sharyn carefully picked her way through the fallen beams and debris. When she was in school, they had dared one another to go into the building. Sharyn had always taken the bet. Until the day her father caught her. The fire department had sealed the place off at one time but through the years, it had become a place for the homeless and teenagers to congregate.

"Sheriff Sharyn Howard," Ernie introduced her as she got close to him and another man. "This is Monty. We were stationed in Nam together for a while."

"Sheriff." The man acknowledged her but didn't look at her.

"Monty."

"Tell her what you told me," Ernie encouraged him.

"You tell her," Monty responded. "I ain't much good at it."

Ernie put his hand on Monty's filthy shoulder. "Monty found something in the Dumpster behind the playhouse."

"Before or after Willy died?"

"After." Monty pitched in, despite his reluctance. "Willy was already dead."

"How did you know it was there?"

"I seen him put it in there a few nights before. People don't go there all the time so it isn't a good place to get stuff but it's a good place to *keep* stuff. If you know what I mean."

"I think I do." Sharyn glanced at Ernie. "What kind of stuff?"

"Missing parts of Edith Randolph's life." He handed her an old brown photo album.

Sharyn glanced at the pictures and newspaper clippings inside the damp, smelly book.

"I just wanted to help Willy." Monty scuffed his old tennis shoe on the blackened concrete.

"But you didn't see anything?" Sharyn asked him.

"Nothing. I didn't touch Willy, either. I hope he gets a decent burial. He deserves a decent burial, Sheriff."

"We'll take care of it, Monty."

"Thanks. I met your daddy once. He shook my hand. He was a good'un."

Sharyn nodded. "Thanks. I guess I'll get this back to the office."

"Stay here a minute, Monty," Ernie told him. "I'll be right back."

"Ernie," Sharyn said, opening the photo album again. "*This* is what was missing!"

"I know, Sheriff. I'm going to give Monty some money. I know that's why he called me—he thought it was worth something. I'll meet you back at the office."

Sharyn dug around in her pocket and came up with twenty dollars. "Here, give him this, too."

"Sheriff—"

She put it into his hand. "Just give it to him. And hurry back."

SHARYN TOLD TRUDY to hold her calls and locked her office door behind her. She sat at her desk, put on a pair of gloves, and looked slowly through the book.

On the first page was a picture of Caison and Edith. She looked like a performer of some sort. She was wearing red feathers and a skimpy gold costume. Her blond hair was piled on her head, her lips were dark red, and she was wearing too much eye shadow.

Caison Talbot was dressed in a polo shirt and khaki pants. His hair was still dark, but turning white in places. He was grinning broadly at the camera. It was difficult to make out what the background was until she turned the page and saw another picture of them together—outside a casino in Las Vegas.

There was a knock on the door and Sharyn hid the book under her desk.

Ernie's worried eyes met hers when she opened the door. "This is big trouble."

"I'm going to call Nick. These are only pictures and newspaper clippings, Ernie. Check with Las Vegas PD. Let's see if Edith Randolph was ever Edith Talbot. While we're waiting for their answer, I think we should go and talk to the senator."

Ernie nodded grimly. "I don't want to say anything in the open office. Too many people. I'm going to let Cari handle this. I think we can trust her."

Sharyn nodded. "Okay. Let's go."

Senator Caison Talbot lived in a huge Victorian home that sat squarely at the edge of Main Street. It had once been Diamond Springs' library, but he had purchased it and refurbished it with his late wife, Marcy.

Sharyn knew that Caison and Marcy were only married for about ten years when Marcy died. The incident with Edith had taken place thirty years before, according to the newspaper clippings. He hadn't been married at the time. There was no reason for anyone to know that he'd had a fling with a show-girl in Las Vegas. If Edith hadn't ended up dead in Diamond Springs, it would have stayed a secret. The question was: why had Edith come to seek him out?

The big, dark car Willy saw at the motel. The tall, thin man who walked past him. What were the chances that he wasn't describing the senator and one of the many cars parked in the garage behind the house?

"Sharyn!" Talbot greeted them at the door. "Deputy Watkins! Come in. This is a surprise."

Faye Howard came down the long flight of rounded stairs, already looking like a queen in her palace. Faye was born to be a senator's wife. "Sharyn! Did you come to bring me my key?"

"Uh—no, Mom. It isn't made yet. I'll try and drop it off later."

Faye glanced at Caison then back at her daughter. "You just dropped by? During working hours?"

"I'm afraid this is work-related," Sharyn told her mother. "We need to have a conversation alone with Senator Talbot."

"Alone?" Faye demanded, drawing herself up to her full petite height. "I don't see any reason for that. Do you, Caison?"

"None whatsoever. Would you like some lemonade or a Coke, Sheriff? Deputy?"

Sloane Phillips joined them in the foyer. "Sheriff. Can I get you something?"

"No, thanks, Mr. Phillips."

"We need to speak with the senator privately," Ernie reiterated.

"Nonsense!" Caison objected. "Faye and I are going to be married. Sloane has been with me for a long time. I trust both of them with whatever you plan to tell me. Let's go into the library."

The library was a huge, impressive, two-story

room with a rounded ceiling. Books crammed shelves on all the walls and a fireplace sat filled with fresh flowers in one corner. The furniture was overstuffed, wine-colored velvet. Caison and Faye sat on the love-seat with their hands entwined. Sloane took a chair by the window, leaving Ernie and Sharyn to share the loveseat across from the couple.

"Senator, we need to talk again about what happened the day you were shot." Sharyn looked at her mother uncomfortably.

"I don't think he really remembers, Sharyn," her mother answered for him, the way she'd always answered for T. Raymond.

"Mom, please."

Ernie took up the questioning. "Senator, what *can* you recall about that day?"

"As I told the sheriff," Caison said, his tone becoming imperious, "I went to the old mill to look around. I heard a noise and I felt something sting my arm. I realized that I had been shot and fell back into the corn chute."

"Why the corn chute?" Sharyn asked.

"It was an old trick we used to do when we were kids. There are places in there where air pockets occur. I guess I passed out after I got in there."

"So you felt that someone might still be after you?"

"Yes, Deputy! I *had* just been shot!"

"But you didn't see anyone?"

"No. I didn't see anyone in the loft with me, but there were plenty of people on the ground floor."

"We found your car in the woods a few miles away," Sharyn told him. "It was smashed with a hammer."

"Vandals."

"Or someone who really hates you."

Talbot glared at Sharyn. "As I told you before, it would be a miracle if people didn't hate me in this job! I get death threats all the time."

"Would you mind if we took a look at some of them?"

"Sloane handles that," Caison told them.

"I'll be glad to help out however I can," Sloane chipped in.

Sharyn stared at the senator. "What do you know about a woman named Edith Randolph?"

"Who?"

"Edith Randolph. She was from Nebraska, but she arrived here in Diamond Springs about a week ago."

"I've never heard of her." He looked at Sloane for help. "Does that name sound familiar to you?"

"No, sir."

Sharyn passed the senator a picture of Edith from the motel room. "She was killed late Saturday night. Smothered in her motel room."

Caison glanced at it. "I heard about it. Grisly affair. But I don't know her."

Sharyn took out another picture, the one of Caison and Edith together in Las Vegas. "Look again, Senator. You did know Edith Randolph."

"Do you have my glasses, Sloane?"

"Here they are, sir."

Caison looked carefully at the picture. "I don't recall this, Sheriff. Did this woman say she knew me?"

Faye looked at the picture. "Sharyn, this could be one of those pictures like they use in those tabloids!"

"True enough," Sharyn agreed, taking the pictures back from them. "But I should warn you, sir, that a man claimed to have seen a tall, thin man with a large, dark car come out of Edith Randolph's room the night she was killed."

"Did he say it was me?"

"No, sir."

"Are you telling me he saw me but he didn't know who I was?" he demanded. "Sheriff, if he lives in Diamond Springs, he knows me."

"He was a homeless man, Senator. I don't know how well he kept up with the news."

"Well, where is he?" Caison asked. "Let him identify me now!"

"Unfortunately," Ernie intervened, "he's dead also. Shot down behind the playhouse."

"So, on the basis of this rather loose testimony from a man who's now dead—a homeless man at that—who didn't even know me even though my face is everywhere, and from these pictures that may or may not be me, you want to accuse me of murder?"

"No, sir," Sharyn retaliated. "We want to know the truth."

Caison rose to his full height, towering over Sharyn. "Young woman, don't start a witch hunt you can't support! I know this is an election year, and you don't look so good with two murders that you can't solve. But don't run up against *me!* You won't win!"

He left the room. Faye got up to follow him. "I can't believe you would do this, Sharyn! How low will you stoop?"

"Mom—"

Faye turned her back and followed the senator out of the room.

Sloane rose quietly from his chair. "I know this must be some mistake, Sheriff. The senator does have enemies. I can make those letters available to you."

"Thanks," she replied. "You mentioned at the hospital that the senator was acting strangely before he was shot. Has that continued?"

Sloane glanced at the empty doorway, clearly torn between his loyalty to the senator and the truth. "I think the senator is concerned about his health, Sheriff. As I told you at the hospital."

"Had he been ill before the shooting?" Sharyn asked him.

"He'd had some tests done, but nothing showed up."

"Sloane!" the senator bellowed.

"Excuse me, Sheriff. Deputy."

"That went well," Ernie remarked as they left the house together.

"Yeah," Sharyn agreed. "Is my head still on my shoulders?"

"Yeah, but those red curls are a little blackened from the fire he was belching out!"

"He's right, Ernie. We don't have enough to bring him in for questioning, much less convict him of anything."

"We don't have enough to *arrest* him, Sheriff. Quit thinking like a lawyer!"

Nick was waiting back at the office. Ed and Joe were just coming in from a call. They converged in the conference room with Cari.

"Well?" Nick asked.

Sharyn passed the photo book to him.

"Have you been handling this without gloves?"

"It's thirty years old," Ernie argued.

"Come on, Ernie! It was at the scene of a murder!"

"Any forensic evidence that would have been on that book is in the trash can!"

Nick handled the book with a glove that Cari got for him from the evidence room. "I can't believe you guys didn't think about it!"

"Thirty years doesn't mean anything to fingerprints and DNA," Cari quipped.

"Thanks." Nick glanced at her. "What's inside anyway?"

"Pictures of Caison Talbot and Edith Randolph," Sharyn told him.

"Are they engraved or something? How did you think you were going to make a case against him with this?"

"Nick!"

He stood up. "I'm taking this back to my office. I'll let you know when I'm done with it."

"Somebody's touchy," Ed whispered as they watched Nick stalk out of the sheriff's office.

"It's not easy to lose out," Joe reminded him.

"Anyway." Sharyn brought them back to the issue at hand. "The photo book does have pictures of Talbot and our murdered lady together in Las Vegas thirty years ago."

"And—I've got a wedding license for them from Las Vegas." Cari played her trump card with a flourish. "I also received an annulment notice from three days later."

"You did good, Cari!" Ernie beamed at his protégé. "Who filed for the annulment?"

"Caison Emmet Talbot." She produced the second paper.

"She didn't have time to change her driver's license," Ernie whispered.

"I hate this," Ed proclaimed.

"Okay, they were married." Joe got everyone's attention away from the two documents. "Why did he kill her?"

"Why did she come here when she knew she was dying?" Cari countered.

"She was still in love with him all these years," Ernie hypothesized. "She was dying. She wanted to see him one last time."

"She made it to the motel and called him. He came over and smothered her," Joe said.

Sharyn disagreed. "But he wasn't married at the time he married her. There wasn't anything illegal about what he did. With the clout Talbot has around here, he wouldn't be worried enough about someone finding out that he had married and divorced a show-girl thirty years ago to kill her."

"No but it would be embarrassing," Ed continued. "I don't think the senator would risk everything because he might be *embarrassed*."

"We *are* just seeing what was in that book," Ernie reminded her. "Maybe something more happened, and she was the only one who knew about it."

Sharyn shook her head. "You mean like they killed someone or robbed a bank?"

"I believe Willy was telling the truth," Ernie defended the man. "I think he did see a tall, thin man with a large, dark car."

"And I checked the DMV records," Cari added.

"There are two sedans registered to him. One black. The other burgundy. Either one could have looked dark at night."

Sharyn took it all in with an unwilling ear. "What about the senator's argument? His face is on signs all over the county!"

"But Willy would have been as likely to notice that as you would be to notice a flea on the ground! He didn't care about politics," Ernie rebutted.

"But doesn't it make great reading that he died possessing the photo book with the incriminating pictures?" Ed grinned.

"Before we go any further, we need to know a few things," Sharyn told them. "First of all, we need to know if the senator has a gun that matches the weapon that killed Willy, and we need to have it tested. Quietly, if possible. Next, we need to see if Las Vegas PD can track any of his movements when he was there."

Ernie asked, "Have we given up on the idea that Edith might have a son who could shed some light on all of this?"

"No," Sharyn replied. "We haven't. In fact, check it out with this new evidence. We couldn't find any record of a son born to Edith Randolph, but what about Edith Talbot?"

Ernie stopped short at the suggestion. Then he nodded. "I'm on it. Coming, partner?"

Cari got up. "I'll check with Las Vegas again."

"What do you want us to do?" Joe asked.

"Have Ernie check to see if the senator has a gun registered. If he does, go over to his house and try to pick it up to have it tested."

"If he doesn't want to do it?"

She shrugged. "We'll get a warrant and the fat will hit the fire!"

Ed got up from his chair. "And you'll smooth things over with Nick, and find out what bee is in his bonnet now, right?"

Sharyn nodded. "You got it."

She closed up her file and told Trudy where she was going. It was cooler outside after the storm. The air was still a little misty. The walk helped to clear her head. She was feeling the effects of being up and running all night long. The adrenaline was wearing off, and all that was left was a dull ache behind her eyes.

Nick was working on the photo book when she walked into his basement office in the hospital. Megan and Keith were there, along with about ten other students of various ages. He was explaining each process he used as he went along. The students were so wrapped up in what he was saying, that no one noticed when she walked into the room.

"Don't come in without gloves, goggles and a gown," he said to her without looking up.

Sharyn frowned. He'd noticed that she was there

but obviously wasn't pleased by it. The students all looked up at her.

"I'll wait in your office, *Dr.* Thomopolis."

He looked up then, but Sharyn was gone.

Sharyn decided to stand while she waited for him. If she sat in his chair or on the sofa, she was afraid she'd fall asleep. Her brain was going through the motions, but her body was dragging behind.

Nick came in behind her and closed the door. "I've got a copy of the senator's prints, but I don't think we're going to get a positive ID from that book. It was definitely handled by Edith Randolph. There's a strand of hair I've isolated, though I don't know if it matters. It wasn't hers or Willy's. Between the garbage and the bad handling, it could have come from anyone."

She took a deep breath. "All right, thanks. Ed and Joe went out to pick up the senator's gun, if he has one. Would you like to take a look at that, or would you like me to take it to Harold?"

"Either way," Nick remarked. "I've done everything I can do until we get the muskets back. I'm only working on this book."

"Any word on the muskets?"

"I called and got his answering machine. Maybe I'll take a run down there this weekend if I don't hear from him."

"Nick—"

"I'm sorry, Sharyn. I didn't mean to blow up. I'm tired. Ed and Cari were talking about you and David having some kind of secret rendezvous. You're right—this isn't going to work." He sat on the corner of his desk and looked at the floor.

"Well, that was pretty short, even for us," she said carefully. She cleared her throat. "I have to get back to the office. If Talbot won't turn over the gun voluntarily, I'll get a warrant for it."

"The press will eat that up. You've done a good job of keeping it quiet so far."

"Thanks. And thanks for your help last night." She put her hand on the doorknob to walk out.

"Don't leave."

She froze next to the door. "Nick—"

"I can handle the part where you don't want anyone to know. I just can't handle hearing the gossip whispering about you and David, like I think it's great that the two of you are in love."

Sharyn didn't turn around. "It's kind of funny, isn't it? All this time, they've been whispering about me and you."

"Sharyn, I—"

"I have to get back," she told him quietly. She opened the door and walked out of the office.

"Professor Thomopolis?" Keith called out. "I think we might have found another print."

"Great," Nick muttered darkly. "I'm coming."

SHARYN REFUSED TO think about the situation with Nick, whatever it was. She had too many other things on her mind.

Ed called her cell phone as she was walking back to the sheriff's office. "He has two guns registered to him, Sheriff. A .45 Firestorm and a 9 mm Medusa. We're at his house. He won't give the Firestorm up without a warrant."

Sharyn leaned against the side of a building for a moment and stared up at the overcast sky. More storms were coming. She could see the feeder clouds above the mountains. "I'll call the D.A., Ed. Stay where you are. I know I don't have to tell you that we are 'no comment' on any of this."

"No problem, Sheriff."

She called Jack Winter and spoke to his assistant, Lennie.

"You want a search warrant to get a gun that's registered to the senator? Do you think he killed someone?"

"I think he may have been involved in the killing of Willy Newsome."

"I'll tell Mr. Winter," Lennie promised. "Hold on a minute."

Sharyn waited patiently on the street corner.

Lennie finally came back. "Mr. Winter says he can have it to you within the hour."

"Thanks, Lennie," she responded. "We're trying to keep this low profile."

"I understand, Sheriff."

Sharyn closed her cell phone. It was useless saying that they could keep it low profile—the press would sniff out something like this. By the time they had the search warrant, reporters would be at the senator's door.

"Sheriff!" Cari called as she reached the office. "We've got something!"

Sharyn was glad that someone was eager to find out more about this case, and she could see by the look on Ernie's face that he felt the same way.

"There's no record of the senator doing anything but getting married and separated during the time he spent in Las Vegas," Cari chirped happily. "There's no record of a baby born to Edith Randolph or Talbot going back twenty years. That's as far back as their computers go."

"He was there thirty years ago, Cari," Sharyn reminded her. "They'll have to do a physical search for it."

The young deputy drooped visibly.

"But you did very well."

"Thanks, Sheriff."

Ernie walked with Sharyn to her office. "Did they have to get a warrant for the gun?"

"Yes."

"Idiot!" Ernie said beneath his breath. "He's only making it harder on himself."

"If he has nothing to hide."

"Even if he does have something to hide! He knows how the law works!"

"He's probably already on the phone with his lawyer."

"Who do you think it will be?"

She shrugged. "I might have said Eldeon Percy, but since he was representing Willy, that would be a conflict."

"What did Nick have to say?"

Sharyn sank down gratefully in the chair behind her desk. "He said he's trying to isolate a strand of hair from the book, but it's a mess because someone didn't handle it the right way."

Ernie shrugged. "I didn't think there would be anything on it after all this time and the way it's been treated. Monty slept on it the last few nights."

"It might not be anything, Ernie. You know how Nick gets sometimes. I'm just as bad. I didn't think about it, either. I was so worried about what was inside that I didn't think about fingerprints or DNA."

"I guess that's why he's the medical examiner and we're the law."

Sharyn told him about finding Jack Winter in her house that morning. Ernie watched her play with the new keys to the house that Dewey, their handyman, had left for her while she was out.

"My Dad and Jack Winter. How close were they, Ernie?"

He'd been dreading that question. "Not as close as your daddy and I were, but as close as he was to anyone else he worked with."

"Didn't he realize what kind of man he was?"

"I don't know, Sheriff. We never talked about it."

Sharyn sat back in her chair and looked at the ceiling. "Every time something comes up with Jack Winter or Caison Talbot, I get this awful feeling that I'm going to find out something really bad about my father. Is there any truth to that, Ernie?"

He considered her question carefully. "If there is, I don't know about it."

"That will have to be good enough for me. If I am reelected sheriff, I'm going after the D.A. and the rest of the power brokers in Diamond Springs."

"I don't know about T. Raymond," he cautioned, "but you might not like other things you'll find."

"I can't stand not knowing, and wanting to run and hide every time I think Dad's name might be part of an investigation."

"I don't blame you. But I don't believe T. Raymond did anything you have to worry about."

"Thanks, Ernie. I hope you're right."

SHARYN GAVE A speech before the League of Women
Voters later that day. The women were happy to have
her there. They were a supportive and friendly group
who welcomed her without reserve. They asked her
questions about her job and what it was like to make
a decision to use a firearm. She answered as best she
could and they asked her to come back after the election to give her victory speech.

She called into the office on her way home. Cari
and Ernie were still waiting for more information
on the case. Nick hadn't called with anything else.

Ed and Joe hadn't been able to find the .45 Firestorm after they'd received the warrant to search the
senator's home. The story made the midday news as
the press speculated why a warrant to search Talbot's
home had been issued. Her deputies were as discreet
as ever with the press yelling in their faces. Trudy
warned her that Foster Odom was looking for her.

Sharyn met Don James for another coaching ses-
sion. He didn't like the way she walked and wanted
her to speak with less of a Southern accent. He told
her that he'd scheduled three more speeches that week
at Rotary Clubs around the county. The following
week was her first debate with Roy Tarnower. She
would have to be carefully coached for that one. She
was too tired to take it all in while she was with him,
so she just smiled and nodded a lot.

When she got home, she checked and rechecked

the locks on the doors. Then she tried to forget about Jack Winter being there. She looked at everything in the house but there was no sign that he'd taken anything. She wondered why he'd really been there that day. Had her father been holding some papers for him?

Faye wouldn't return her phone calls. Apparently, Sharyn had finally gone one step too far. Selma let Kristie call her, but after talking to her sister, she felt even more alone in the empty house.

Sharyn took a hot bath and almost fell asleep in the tub. Afterwards, she pulled on her old robe and wadded her hair up in a towel. She looked through her mother's facial products and slathered a mask on her face, then made a bowl of popcorn and propped herself in front of the television. She was watching the news when a bulletin came up on the screen.

"In a late-breaking story tonight, District Attorney Jack Winter has released the information that Senator Caison Talbot from Diamond Springs is being sought for the recent murders of two people in that area. Senator Talbot was unavailable for comment."

EIGHT

SHARYN WAS AT the District Attorney's office at seven the next morning. She clipped on her badge and holstered her grandfather's gun. She was furious and wanted some answers.

After wading through reporters to reach the courthouse, she took the elevator to Jack Winter's office. "Is he in?"

"Yes, but—"

Sharyn didn't wait for Lennie's reply. She pushed open the doors to the opulent interior office and confronted her nemesis.

A sleazy-looking man jumped up from his chair and started to pull out a gun.

"Max!" Winter cautioned.

"I hope you have a permit for that, sir," Sharyn addressed the man. "Of course, what's interesting is how it made it past the metal detectors at the front door."

"Max came in through the back stairs," Jack Winter explained. "He works for me as a private detective."

"I see."

"It was Max who found what you were looking for yesterday, Sheriff."

"What's that?"

"The senator's gun, of course." The D.A. turned to his hired hand. "I'll talk to you later, Max. Good job."

"Thanks." Max looked at Sharyn. "Nice meeting you, Sheriff."

When Max left, Lennie came bustling into the room, asking if either of them wanted anything to drink.

"No, thanks," Sharyn refused.

"We're fine, Lennie, thank you."

Lennie shrugged his broad shoulders, flashed his Super Bowl ring, and straightened his Armani suit. "I'll just be out here, sir, if you need me."

"Yes, fine, Lennie."

The door closed behind him. Winter smiled at Sharyn. "Alone at last!"

"Where did Max find the gun?"

"Actually, there's an interesting story that goes with it."

Sharyn didn't smile. "Where, sir?"

He frowned. "You seem a little hostile this morning, Sharyn."

"You announced to the news media last night that we were going to arrest Caison Talbot for murder. You made it sound like he was a fugitive! I didn't realize that's what we were doing."

"Sharyn—"

"Where do you get your information? From people like Max?"

"I keep my ear to the ground. You can't be successful if you don't. I'm sure you don't need me to tell you that! And you know how the media can twist your words."

"Then your ear should have told you that we haven't finished the investigation. There hasn't been an arrest warrant issued for Senator Talbot."

"I knew you were missing this key piece of evidence." He produced a gun wrapped in plastic and set it on his desktop.

"How do we know that's the senator's gun?"

"You already know he has a .45 Firestorm registered to him. Have Dr. Thomopolis check it out. If the senator has ever used it, his prints should be on it. If not, then he can check it to see if it's the murder weapon."

Sharyn took a deep breath. "Where was it found?"

"In a private trash can about a block from the playhouse. I checked. It's registered to Caison."

She nodded and started to reach for it. He put his hand on hers when she'd grabbed the gun.

"Sharyn, this represents a unique opportunity for you. The only one of its kind."

She sat very still and didn't move her hand. "I think there are plenty of guns out there, sir."

He smiled. His eyes searched her face. "It's not the gun. It's the *opportunity*."

Her skin was beginning to crawl, but she didn't want to give him the upper hand. "The opportunity to catch whoever killed Willy Newsome?"

"Compared to where you could be, that's struggling through the dirt! You're a woman of rare judgment and perception. I see so much in you. You're strong and you don't mind taking chances. I want you on my side."

Sharyn sat forward in her chair. She decided that she'd put up with this man for too long. "Sir, I will *never* be on your side. You're a metaphor for everything that's wrong with Diamond Springs. If I lose this election and I'm not sheriff for another term, I'll go back and pass the Bar. And I'll use *that* position to fight you. I hope there's no misunderstanding between us."

Jack Winter looked at her with something close to admiration in his cold eyes. He moved his hand away from hers and sat back in his chair. "There's not a man in this town that would say that to me."

"That's a pity." She picked up the gun and got to her feet. "I don't know what game you're playing in all of this, but there's one thing I do know."

He smiled patronizingly. "What's that, Sharyn?"

"I'll beat you at it. Have a good day, sir."

He watched her walk out of his office with her

shoulders back and her head high. He had never wanted to control a woman more in his life. He wanted to see her grovel. But she was too much like her father. It had seemed amusing at the time to allow her to become sheriff, but it wasn't funny anymore.

"Lennie," he called to his aide, "get Max back over here. We haven't finished our business."

"Yes, sir."

SHARYN TOOK THE gun directly to Nick. She sat on a stool in a gown, goggles and gloves while he looked at it. Trudy called to tell her that the press was waiting for her to make a statement. The D.A.'s pronouncement had become a media circus. No one had seen Senator Talbot since the news release but his lawyer had called to let them know that he was waiting to hear from them.

"Are you sure you don't want to take this to Harold?"

"No. I want you to do it," she replied.

He'd shrugged and checked the gun for prints. Sharyn shot the gun in the lab. With the captured bullet, they came back to compare the bullets he'd taken from Willy's body.

Sharyn sat silently through the entire process. Nick was unnerved by the quiet. He'd barked at Keith and Megan when they'd come to help, so they'd left the two of them alone and gone back to entering information into the computer.

"You know, you *can* speak," Nick told Sharyn.

"I know. I didn't want to disturb you."

"I'm not disturbed."

"You sounded like it just then," she mocked him.

"They get in the way sometimes. I know this is important to you."

"Oh."

Nick tried to keep his mind on what he was doing, but it wandered back to her. "Where were you last night?"

"At home."

"I called you around ten. There was no answer."

"I fell asleep after the news. It was either that or explode after Winter's announcement."

"I saw that. He's taking it right out of your hands, isn't he?"

"I don't know *what* he's doing."

"I thought he and the senator were big buddies."

"They are. Or they were. I don't know."

He shook his head. "The senator's prints are all over this gun. The bullet matches the bullets that killed Willy Newsome. You don't get much more of a solid case than this."

Sharyn nodded. "I'm going to have to bring him in for questioning. I don't have any choice."

Nick laughed. "Don't tell me. You don't think he did it?"

"Not for any reason I've heard so far," she answered.

"He's a proud man, Sharyn." Nick switched off the overhead light. "If this woman really had something that could hurt him, it could have been enough to drive him over the edge."

"My father told me once that it's more important to know your enemies than it is to know your friends," she explained. "I think this applies here. I just can't imagine Caison Talbot doing more than laughing off this whole thing."

"I realize the D.A. has put you into a bad position, but you can keep investigating."

"I will." She smiled at him without really seeing him. "Thanks, Nick."

"Sharyn?"

"Hmm?"

He took off his gloves and touched her arm. "When this is over, before another catastrophe hits this town, we have to talk."

"Nick, I think we've said it all, haven't we?"

"No. I can still feel it, *here*—" he touched his chest "—between us."

"I won't let it come between us if you won't," she promised. "It's taken us a long time to learn to work together. Call me on my cell phone if anything else shows up."

"Yeah, sure."

SHARYN WALKED TO the senator's gingerbread house on the corner. The lawn was thick with reporters, but there were security guards at the fence.

"Sheriff!" Foster Odom hailed her from the street. "If I could just have a word with you—"

"After that interview you published yesterday, Mr. Odom?" she queried coldly. "Be glad I'm not arresting you for jaywalking!"

"That's harsh, Sheriff," he protested. "I only call them as I see them."

She smiled at him. "I hope you've got good eyes then, Mr. Odom, because you'll be calling them about me from a far greater distance!"

He backed off as he opened the gate to the senator's yard. Apparently the security people had set the fence as a perimeter.

"Excuse me—" the first guard accosted her "—this is private property."

"Do I look like a reporter to you?" she asked the man. "I'm the sheriff of Montgomery County. Step aside, sir."

The security guard stepped to one side and nodded to her. He spoke to another guard through his radio.

The second security guard met her at the door.

"Senator Talbot has informed us that he isn't taking visitors, ma'am."

Sharyn was fed up with this treatment. "I'm here on official sheriff's business. I'm not *asking* to see the senator. Tell him that he either sees me now or I come back with a warrant for his arrest. This is a courtesy call."

The second security guard waved her through after relaying the information.

Sloane opened the door for her. "Sheriff."

"Mr. Phillips."

"What can I do for you, Sheriff Howard?" Alan Michaelson, the former A.D.A. for Diamond Springs, greeted her.

"Mr. Michaelson! It's been a long time. I was wondering what happened to you." Actually, she had a pretty good idea of what had happened to him. He'd had his eyes on Jack Winter's job and the D.A. had cut him down when he'd made mistakes during Beau Richmond's murder investigation.

He smiled. "When Mr. Winter asked for my resignation, Mr. Percy took me on as a junior partner. I've been at the branch office in Raleigh, but I'm back for the senator."

"Then I know he's in good hands."

"What can I do for you?" he repeated.

"I want to see Senator Talbot. This is a courtesy call, Mr. Michaelson. You know how it works. The senator is about to be arrested for murder. Before that happens, I'd like a chance to talk with him and convince him to give himself up."

Michaelson nodded. "I do know how it works, Sheriff. More importantly, I know how *you* work. I'll recommend that the senator talk with you. But I want to be there to monitor that conversation."

She shrugged. "Fair enough. We don't have a lot of time."

"I'll speak with him."

Sloane showed Sharyn to a sitting room with carefully collected antique furniture. She sat down gingerly on a chair that had spindly legs and pink brocade cushions.

"What do you make of all this, Mr. Phillips?" she asked Caison's aide. "You've been with the senator for a long time—you must have some opinion."

Sloane paused as he was about to leave the room. His good-looking face wore the same air of discomfort as if she'd presented him with a hedgehog for breakfast. "Sheriff—"

"No one is questioning your loyalty, sir. But you do know the senator better than most."

"I—I don't know—"

"If it helps, I don't think he's guilty of these murders. There might be something you could tell me that could help me find the real killer."

"I think something's wrong," he confided finally,

his words a whoosh of relief. "I think the senator does know something about what's happened. Not that he hurt anyone— I'd never believe that! It's just that he's so closed off right now. He can't recall things that just happened yesterday. He's under some terrible strain."

"But you think it started a while ago?"

"I do, Sheriff. He has always been so organized, so efficient. But it was there before he came back to Diamond Springs to campaign. As you know, I usually stay behind at the Capitol to see to his affairs. He begged me to come with him this time. He said he didn't want to be alone. I heard him say the same thing to your mother."

Suddenly the door burst open, and Senator Talbot strode into the room. Sloane disappeared quickly with a last desperate look at Sharyn.

"Well, Sheriff Howard. You've come to arrest me?" the senator demanded.

Michaelson took a seat on another spindly chair, while Caison seated himself on the narrow sofa. Faye followed him quickly into the room.

Sharyn shook her head. "Mom, you're making this harder!"

"Sharyn," her mother rebuked her regally, "I will be here as long as Caison wants me here."

"Okay. I don't have a lot of time, and there's no point arguing."

Faye glared at her daughter with unforgiving eyes. "You've gone too far this time, Sharyn!"

The sheriff of Montgomery County ignored her mother. There was nothing she could say that would convince her that she had Talbot's best interests at heart. She focused on the senator, who was looking a little frail and worn to her eyes. "Senator, I don't mean any disrespect by being here. I hope you know that. I'm here because you're about to be arrested for murder."

Caison stared at her. His eyes were so blue in his white face that Sharyn felt chilled by them.

"So you're not here to arrest me?"

"No, sir."

"How did that come about?"

"Because Jack Winter is after your head, sir. I don't know why. I never issued any statement to him about the murder investigation. Everything he's done has been independent of my office. He gave me a gun he said was yours. It's registered to you. I had it tested by Nick Thomopolis."

"And?" Michaelson prompted.

"The bullet matched the bullets found in Willy Newsome's body."

"No one is going to believe I knew a homeless alcoholic, Sheriff! I appreciate your concern, but—"

"Senator, listen for once in your life! This crime

links you to the murder of Edith Randolph at the
Bridge Motel. It gives you motive."

"He already told you he doesn't know that woman,"
her mother added.

"He was married to her!" Sharyn answered sharply.
"We have the marriage license and the annulment papers. I have to assume by now that the D.A. has those
papers, as well. He seems to have a way of finding
out what he needs to know."

"Caison?" Faye questioned in a faint voice. "Is
this true?"

Talbot shook his head. "This is preposterous! I
never heard such a rag of lies and deceptions!"

There was a knock at the door, accompanied by a
call from the security guard outside.

Michaelson looked at Sharyn. "It seems that two
of your deputies are here to arrest the senator."

Sharyn nodded to Caison, "Get him out of here."

"What?" the ex-A.D.A. asked in disbelief.

"I don't know what the D.A. has in store for him,
but I know it's not good. And you know Jack Winter well enough to know how *he* works, too, Mr. Michaelson!"

"But you're the sheriff," Michaelson floundered,
"and I'm an officer of the court!"

"So far as I know at this moment," Sharyn confided, "there hasn't been an arrest warrant issued for

the senator. If your radio had been working, we might have known better."

He nodded mutely.

"Get him out of here!"

Sloane rushed to the senator's side when they opened the sitting room door. Faye stood beside him, though she looked bewildered and lost. "There's a car around back. We can take the side street."

Michaelson nodded to Sharyn as they walked out the back door. When it had closed behind them and she'd watched the dark sedan pull away from the house, she opened the front door.

"Sheriff!" Ernie studied her closely. "What are you doing here? We tried to call you!"

"What's happened?" she asked coolly, for the benefit of the reporters and the security guards.

"There's been an arrest warrant issued for Caison Talbot," Ed replied briskly.

Both men looked at her, unsure how to proceed. Time seemed suspended, like the heat waves floating in the summer air around them.

"He's not here," Sharyn told them. "He wasn't feeling well. They took him to the hospital."

Ernie breathed a sigh of relief. "I guess we'll go there for him then, huh?"

"He won't be going anywhere for a while."

He squinted at her, trying to figure out what was going on. The warrant had bypassed them entirely.

It had been issued by the D.A. The sheriff not being there had made him even more uncomfortable. "Yes, ma'am."

"We'll talk when you bring him back to the office."

Ed nodded and walked back to the car with Ernie. The reporters, who'd seemed as stagnant as water in an old birdbath, were now moving fast, trying to reach the hospital before the deputies.

"What just happened back there, Ernie?" Ed asked him.

"I don't know yet. But I can tell you one thing."

"What's that?"

"Sharyn is the worst liar in the universe! Come on, let's go to the hospital."

Sharyn walked through the crowd, ignoring the reporters who, for the most part, ignored her. Their quarry and the big story were at the hospital. The senator's lawn emptied quickly.

She felt as if she didn't breathe until she walked into the sheriff's office. There was a moment of silence when she entered.

Joe followed her into her office. "What's going on? Winter is executing orders for an arrest we haven't even processed. You disappear all morning. I feel like I'm in a bad late-night movie!"

"I don't know what's going on yet, Joe," she confided. "But I don't want to talk about it now."

"Oh, that's just great! Can we talk about it tomorrow at Tara?"

Sharyn put her hand to her forehead. It was starting to hurt and it wasn't even lunchtime. But that gave her an idea. "Ernie and Ed should have the senator processed by lunchtime, so we can still have our picnic."

"What?" He looked at her as though she'd lost her mind.

"Our picnic at the park that we were planning today. Why don't you give Ernie and Ed a call as you're leaving the office?"

He scratched his head. Maybe he *was* in a bad late-night movie. "Sure. I'll radio them and—"

"Use your cell phone. Call their cell phones. Don't use the radio."

Joe smiled and backed out of the office. "You're makin' me feel real spooky here, Sheriff. Maybe you need to lie down for a while. It's hot out and—"

"Joe, get Cari and meet me at the park! That's an order!"

"Yes, ma'am!"

Sharyn got in her Jeep and called Nick at the hospital. "I'm swinging by the hospital to pick you up in about five minutes. Be there!"

Nick looked at his phone as it went dead in his hand.

ERNIE AND ED were the last ones to arrive at Palmer Park, one of the few places in Diamond Springs

whose name hadn't been changed when old man
Palmer had died in the '50s.

Nick, Cari, Sharyn and Joe were already at the
picnic shelter that overlooked the lake.

"Will someone please tell me what's going on
today?" Ernie demanded. "First, the D.A. issues an
arrest warrant without us, then the sheriff sends us
on a wild-goose chase to the hospital to pick up the
senator, who was never even there! Now we're pic-
nicking in the park? Is it the heat? Has everyone lost
their minds?"

"Sit down, Ernie," Sharyn said, sliding over on the
bench so he could sit beside her.

"The sheriff was just filling us in on what's happened today," Joe told them. "It's not good."

Ed took his seat and looked down at the empty
table. "Where's lunch?"

Joe smiled and Cari giggled. Nick grinned and
rubbed his hands across his eyes. Ernie's face wid-
ened with laughter. He poked Sharyn in the side and
she shook her head, smiling too.

Ed looked bewildered. "What?"

"Now *there's* a man who has his priorities straight,"
Ernie complimented.

"Okay." Sharyn looked at her deputies. "Maybe
this does seem a little strange."

"A little?" Nick hounded her.

"Okay, a *lot* strange! And if one of you can tell me

how Jack Winter gets his information without having the office bugged or hacking into our computers, I'll feel really silly being here. If not, then you have to know that something is wrong."

Ernie groaned. "Here it comes."

"Think about it, Ernie! Caison Talbot is too big for anything this petty. He'd ride through an affair with a showgirl like most of us would glide through water. He wasn't married, he had a fling that didn't work out. He wouldn't have killed Edith Randolph to keep her from talking about it."

"I can't believe you're defending him, Sheriff." Ed stared at her. "You two have never been friends."

"There's a world of difference between not being friends and standing by while the D.A. sets up him up for murder!"

"What makes you say that?" Cari questioned, wide-eyed to have been included in this meeting.

"Winter gave me the gun his hired hand found. He told me it was found in a trash can a few blocks from Willy's murder scene. It belongs to Talbot. He told me to have Nick check it out, but he already knew the results! He issued the order for Talbot's arrest just a few minutes after I left Nick."

"I didn't send him anything," Nick said stoically.

"Exactly! He set the whole thing up by announcing last night that we were looking for the senator for murder. He knew I'd show up this morning to give him a hard time. He gave me the gun, then he started proceedings against Talbot."

Joe ran his hand through his dark, closely cropped hair. "What about the gun?"

"It was the gun used to kill Willy," Nick answered. "The senator's prints are all over it."

"And we're sitting here, debating if the D.A. should have issued an arrest warrant?" Ed asked.

"Ed, the senator and Jack Winter have always done *everything* together," Sharyn reminded him. "Do you think the D.A. has suddenly developed a conscience in time to ruin his best friend's life?"

"But the evidence—" Cari floundered when they all looked at her. Her cheeks turned red and hot. "It's very compelling."

"But it doesn't make sense," Sharyn argued.

"I've been here before," Ed noted.

"People do things for illogical reasons," Cari returned. "Like the victim coming to Diamond Springs when she was dying."

"There's more to it than that," Sharyn said.

Nick shook his head. "I'm getting too old for this."

Ed laughed. "Yeah, me too! This used to be a simple job. Nothing made any sense and no one cared."

"It's that college education," Ernie teased. "If she would have studied something else—"

"Like basket weaving or cooking," Nick joined in.

Sharyn's cell phone rang. It was Trudy.

"Sheriff, you might need to come back here quick as you can. The D.A. has made another announcement."

"What is it this time, Trudy?"

"He's announced that he's calling for the senator's late wife to be exhumed."

"Marcy?" Sharyn's awestruck voice suspended all the conversation at the table.

"That's right," Trudy answered. "He says he believes there could be evidence of wrongdoing. He says he's going to be investigating her death as a murder!"

"Thanks, Trudy."

"What is it?" Ernie asked, recognizing the name of Caison's wife.

"The D.A. is calling for Marcy Talbot's body to be exhumed," she told them. "He says he thinks the senator may have murdered her."

SHARYN WAS GRIM and silent as she drove back towards the center of town.

"What are you going to do?" Nick asked carefully.

"I'm going to see the D.A. again."

"And get yourself killed?"

She glanced at him. "Even *you* told me that he's not that obvious! If he killed me right now, everyone would know who did it."

"I'm going with you."

"I'm dropping you off at the hospital."

"Not unless you're prepared to physically kick me out of the Jeep," he warned her.

Sharyn frowned when she looked back at the street. "What happened to you being *laconic?* I don't think this qualifies."

"You," he answered simply. "You happened. And you keep happening. Unless I give up my job, move to Alaska, and generally ruin my life, I'm stuck with you."

She bit her lip as she turned the Jeep around a corner and into the parking lot at the courthouse. "You make it sound about as appetizing as an autopsy."

When she switched off the engine, Nick took her hand. "Look at me, Sharyn, please."

Sharyn looked up at him, embarrassed that her eyes were burning with unshed tears. "I know this can't work between us, Nick. It isn't a big deal."

"It is to me," he whispered. "I can't stay here anymore if I can't be with you. I can't see you every day, pretending that we're not together, without knowing that at some point you're going to be sitting next to me and we're going to be talking about a future of some kind."

"You said—"

"I'm a jerk. It's an unappealing characteristic. Sometimes I fly off the handle. If you don't want to try it with me, I'll understand."

"Nick—"

"But if you think there's *any* chance, I want to try. I can look the other way with David. I can pretend for everyone else that we aren't together, as long as we *are* together."

Sharyn smiled and pushed at her eyes. "Nick, I'm about to tackle Jack Winter. I don't need to be all teary-eyed and mushy! He'll think I like him."

"So? I spilled my guts. Give me some sign, please!"

She leaned close and looked into his dark eyes. Then she meshed her fingers with his. "I think we've been *together* for a while already, we're both just too stubborn to admit it."

Nick kissed her hand. "Okay. Then I want to watch you take on the D.A.!"

Sharyn nodded and slipped out of the Jeep. "Is that why you were going to resign when we worked on that prom murder?"

"Yes."

"What made you change your mind?"

"Because I wasn't going to let some slip of a sheriff run me out of town. I've been happy in Diamond Springs. I realized then who was making me unhappy."

She nodded and stepped into the elevator at the back of the building. She pressed the button as she kissed him quickly. "Stay here!"

The doors closed and Nick slammed his hand into

them. He went to the back stairs, taking them two at a time.

Sharyn stepped out of the elevator and glanced down the hall on the D.A.'s floor. She could hear voices coming from Winter's office. Lennie was gone from his watchdog desk. She walked up to the partially open door and listened.

"You don't want to kill me, Caison, you old fool!"

"You've destroyed my life! You had the *gall* to ask them to dig Marcy up! You're the devil that the tourists talk about here, Jack. Always have been."

"Not always, Caison. You were managing pretty well on your own when I got here. I just refined the process."

"I can still best you," Caison exclaimed. "You can't beat me at my own game! I taught you to play, remember? I sat you down at the table and gave you your stake!"

"It's a case of the student being better than the teacher, old man! Your time is over. Give in gracefully. Put down that gun!"

"Or what?"

Sharyn peered through the crack between the door and the wall. Jack Winter was standing with his back to the window. Caison Talbot was holding a gun on him. Despite the fact that it would be better for her if they both shot each other, the D.A. appeared to be unarmed. She couldn't let the senator shoot him in cold blood.

Quickly, before he had time to notice her, Sharyn threw herself against the senator. He fell to the carpet and she pushed his gun aside. A shot rang out and Jack Winter dropped to the floor behind his desk. The window behind him splintered into a million shards that crystallized in the sunshine that poured in on them.

"I—I can't breathe," the senator wheezed. "I—I can't breathe."

Sharyn moved aside and looked at him. His eyes were rolling back in his head and he was clutching at his chest. She loosened his collar as Nick and Lennie came running in with a security guard from the hallway.

"Call for a paramedic," she yelled to Lennie. "I think he's having a heart attack!"

NINE

Nick knelt down on the other side of the senator. "Start compressions. I'll make sure his airway is clear then count for you."

They worked together on the senator until the paramedics arrived. His heart was beating, but with terrible irregularity. He opened his eyes as they put him on the stretcher and tried to speak to Sharyn but the oxygen mask kept her from hearing him.

"Let me move this a second," she said to the paramedic.

"I can't guarantee—"

"You can't guarantee he's going to live right now," she said. "If he has something to say, I want to hear it."

She carefully moved the mask from his nose and mouth. "Senator? Do you have something you want to say?"

Sharyn had to bend her head almost to his lips to understand his raspy voice. She nodded and put the mask back in place. The paramedics took him quickly out of the room.

"I want twenty-four-hour security on him until he

either dies or goes to jail," Jack Winter barked. "He's obviously become deranged!"

Nick looked at Sharyn and saw a bloodstain spreading across her sleeve. "You've been shot!"

She glanced down at her arm and saw the crease across her sleeve. "The bullet must have clipped me."

"Let's get you to the hospital, too, huh?"

"I'm fine, Nick."

"This is touching," Winter said, straightening his tie. "But can I get back to work now?"

Sharyn stared at him. "Don't you want to know what your friend had to say before he left?"

If he was worried, he didn't show it. Not by a flicker of his eyes or a nervous movement of his hands. "Of course, Sheriff. What did the senator have to say?"

She walked up close to him. Her arm had begun to sting but she ignored it, concentrating on his cold blue eyes and pale face. "He said to ask you how my father died, Mr. Winter."

"The old fool! He's crazy!"

"How *did* my father die?"

"I think you know the answer to that, Sharyn." He leaned close and whispered, "I believe it was the first case you investigated as *sheriff,* wasn't it? You should know the answer better than I."

"If I find out you had anything to do with my father's death—"

"Don't threaten me, Sharyn! Especially not over a dying man's ramblings. I think we both agreed we'd make bad enemies!"

She left the room without another word. When she reached the elevator, she clutched at her arm. "This thing *hurts!*"

"Really?" Nick asked, annoyed that she'd wasted time threatening the D.A. instead of seeing to her own injury. "Let's go back to your office and put a Band-Aid on it."

She glanced at him.

"I'm just kidding! We're going to the hospital. Don't make me start quoting sheriff's regs for you."

"You're so thoughtful!"

"And while we're talking about regs, I think we need a new personal one that fits our new relationship."

"What's that?"

"Don't use your feminine wiles to distract me in the context of our job like you just did with me in the parking lot. You could've been killed going in there by yourself! I could have been your back-up just as well as Ernie or Joe if you'd let me."

Sharyn smiled and tossed him her keys. "I think you should drive. And what about your masculine wiles? Do we have a new, *personal* reg for that?"

He got into the Jeep and started the engine. "We'll have to think about that."

SHARYN WAS IN and out of the emergency room in less than an hour. The bullet had only grazed her arm. It hurt, but it was clean. The doctor bandaged it and gave her a prescription for pain pills. Nick stayed in the room with her while the intern worked nervously on her arm.

She checked on Caison before she left the hospital. There were two security guards at the entrance to intensive care. His doctor told her that the senator had the constitution of a horse, and that the heart attack hadn't been severe.

"I expect he'll be up and walking in a few days. Will he really be going to jail?"

"I don't know yet, sir," she answered truthfully. She handed him a card with her cell phone number on it. "Please call me if his condition changes."

"Sure."

Faye was sitting on a sofa in the waiting room outside of the unit. Selma and Kristie were with her. Kristie jumped up and ran to hug her. Selma followed her with a glance at Sharyn's sleeve.

"Looks like someone winged you."

"The senator. But it was an accident."

"It wouldn't have happened at all if you hadn't done this to him," her mother accused with a catch in her voice.

"I tried to save his life, Mom. He shouldn't have

gone to the D.A.'s office. He should have kept going while we tried to straighten this thing out."

"You think he's innocent?" Selma asked her in disbelief.

Sharyn smiled. "I'm afraid I do."

"As much as you dislike him, that must be a bust!" Kristie declared.

"Not now, Kristie," Selma cautioned.

Nick came and stood beside Sharyn.

Selma looked at them and nodded. "Well, well! It's about time!"

Sharyn glanced at Nick. "I don't know—"

Selma rolled her expressive eyes. "I won't say until you're ready."

"I have to go," Nick told Sharyn. "They're paging me to go to the morgue. Jack Winter didn't waste any time digging up Marcy Talbot's body."

"Let me know if you find anything," Sharyn replied. "*Before* the D.A., if that's possible."

"You got it."

The moment hung between them. Kristie grinned and Selma cleared her throat.

"It won't be a secret for long if you keep looking at each other like that!"

Sharyn and Nick abruptly looked away from each other. Nick muttered his goodbyes and left them.

Kristie giggled. "Sharyn's got a boyfriend."

"Are you coming home yet?" Sharyn asked her

sister, glad to see her looking so well, despite the teasing. Her hair was still purple but she'd taken the ring out of her lip to let it heal.

"Aunt Selma says I'm not through yet," Kristie told her.

"She has to have another three weeks," Selma agreed.

"You should sell that program," Sharyn told her. "You both look great."

Selma hugged Kristie close, then gathered Sharyn into the embrace. "It's called love, darlin'. Take care of that arm. Jacob's got infected once and puffed up twice its size! I've got some plantain poultices that will work wonders, if you need them. You should be drinking some goldenseal tea every day to fight off infection."

"Thanks, Aunt Selma." Sharyn looked at her mother. "Are you taking her under your wing, too?"

"For now. Be careful, Sharyn. Jack can get ugly!"

With Selma's warning in her ears, Sharyn drove back to the office. Ernie and Joe were electronically sweeping the entire place, looking for any piece of hardware that could be helping the D.A. spy on them.

"The place is clean," Ernie told her. "Joe got this equipment from a friend of his in the FBI. There's nothing here except the office videotaping that the state requires. But that's only video, not sound. And not even *good* video! He couldn't so much as read our lips from it."

"Thanks, Ernie. You, too, Joe." She puzzled over his revelation. "So how does he do it?"

"I don't know, Sheriff."

"Sheriff," Trudy called her. "The D.A. is requesting all the files from both murder investigations."

"Tell Lennie I don't know where they are right now but I'll send them over as soon as I find them."

Trudy grinned. "Yes, ma'am."

Ed had taken Cari out on her first patrol. Sharyn questioned Ernie's judgment on that choice, but she didn't comment on it. When she was out of the office, he was in charge. She'd made it a strict policy not to second-guess him.

"So, where are we?" Sharyn asked, sitting down behind her desk.

"About where we were before," Ernie guessed. "What happened up there?"

She explained the events in detail. "The senator told me to ask Winter what happened to T. Raymond."

Ernie's eyes narrowed. "What was that supposed to mean?"

"I don't know. I asked Winter. He said that I investigated the case, I should know better than anyone."

"Talbot was having a heart attack," Joe told her. "You can't expect his words to mean much."

"If he'd died," she reminded him, "his words

would have been deathbed testimony. At the time, he probably thought he was going to die."

"Sheriff, I know it would be nice to blame your daddy's death on a conspiracy between Talbot and Winter, but I don't think it happened that way." Ernie gave her his honest opinion.

"We don't have time for that right now anyway." She pushed herself past her own thoughts. "Nick is doing a postmortem on Marcy Talbot while we're sitting here. Senator Talbot will be taken into custody if he survives. We all know that this is a largely circumstantial case—"

"Except for the senator's gun that killed Willy," Joe added.

"Except for a gun that magically appeared that could have been fired by Winter, for all we know."

"Good luck flying that kite, Sheriff," Ernie said.

"Was there some question about Marcy Talbot's death?" Sharyn asked Ernie.

"I was wondering the same thing. I don't recall anything strange or unusual about her death. Nothing we investigated, anyway. I looked it up over at the *Gazette*. She died while they were on vacation in Colorado from natural causes. There wasn't an autopsy done. Apparently, she'd been at a hospital there. She'd been ill for a while. No one questioned it."

"Let's hope that's all it is." She shook her head. "I

just have a feeling Winter wouldn't play that card if he didn't have something else."

"Sheriff, I don't get it," Joe said, getting to his feet. "I hear it from Ed all the time—Caison Talbot has been involved in lots of dirty deals. None that anyone could prove, but we all know they're out there. He finally gets caught in one and we're trying to prove he didn't do it!"

"I know," Sharyn agreed. "But this doesn't make any—"

"Sense?"

"Exactly. Joe, I don't think Caison did this one."

"What difference does it make? He's dirty. We all know he's dirty. If the D.A. can make the case stick against him, who cares?"

"Why is the D.A. in such a hurry to make this case against him, Joe? He wants to do the right thing? He feels bad because Caison murdered Willy and his ex-wife? I don't think so."

"What's your theory then, Sheriff?"

Sharyn subsided. "I don't think I have one yet. We're still missing some evidence."

"If we wait much longer, the D.A. will have dug up half the town and he'll link the senator to all of their deaths," Ernie added bluntly.

Her cell phone rang. "Sheriff Howard."

"I know what killed Marcy Talbot," Nick spoke without preliminary. "Stomach contents show a huge amount of undigested barbiturates. Probably a bottle or more."

"Could she have been forced to take them?"

"I can't speculate on that, Sharyn. There's no evidence of trauma. I've got a skin and hair test going to the lab. That's about all I can tell you. Offhand, I'd say a suicide. With Winters going after Talbot... if he can make the other charges stick...it's possible someone could see this as questionable."

"Thanks, Nick."

"How's the arm?"

"Sore."

"How about dinner?"

"I don't know." She glanced at Ernie and Joe. "Let me get back to you on that."

"Don't tell me," Ernie said as she closed her phone. "There's evidence of foul play?"

"Nick says under ordinary circumstances it would look like a suicide. Since the D.A. already has Talbot by the throat, who knows?"

"I found it!" Cari yelled. She pounded on the door to Sharyn's office then ran inside. "I found it! It was on my computer when we got back!"

"What?" Joe asked.

"Edith Talbot's baby! She did give birth—to a boy. *In Las Vegas!* Almost nine months to the day after their wedding."

"So he'd be thirty years old now." Joe shrugged.

"What was his name?" Sharyn wondered.

"That's the problem," Cari admitted. "She took the baby home with no given name. He was just baby boy Talbot."

"She named him that even though they were divorced?" Ernie glanced at Sharyn. "Does he know?"

She got to her feet. "Let's see if he's well enough to find out."

"I'll keep looking, Sheriff," Cari promised.

"Good work, Deputy," Sharyn commended. "How was your first patrol?"

"We stopped a speeder on Pine Lake Road. We took a call from a power worker who was stuck on an electrical pole because three kids were playing with his truck. And we answered a call from Diamond Springs High School where the principal is demanding that the two boys who broke a window pay for it."

"Sounds exciting," Sharyn said.

"At least there weren't any stray cows!"

"Let me know if you find out anything more, Cari," Sharyn said.

"JOE'S RIGHT, YOU KNOW," Ernie said when they were in her Jeep. "The senator might have been caught for something he didn't do this time, but it seems fair for him to have to pay the price."

"Not you, too?"

He shrugged. "I'm just saying what everyone else is gonna be thinking."

"Not everyone," she reminded him. "More than half the county voted for him six years ago."

"You know what I mean!"

"I know, Ernie. But we'll have to hope we can catch him at something he *did* do."

He studied her avid face as she drove towards the hospital. "You're *that* sure?"

She nodded. "I'm that sure."

CAISON WAS SITTING up and sipping water from a glass Faye held for him. He'd been moved from intensive care into a private room that had a view of the lake. Sloane Phillips was there with a grave expression on his face.

The doctor nodded to Sharyn and Ernie as they came to the door. "Only a few minutes, please. He's not entirely stable but he's improved a great deal. I'd like to keep him as stress-free as possible."

Sharyn agreed, but looking at the security guards that flanked his room, she knew that wasn't going to be possible. He was wanted for two murders. Three, if the D.A. could make Nick's findings about Marcy into something plausible. He'd threatened Jack Winter with a gun and got off a shot in a government building. Stress was going to be a certainty during the next few weeks.

She looked at him talking quietly with his aide while her mother held his hand. He looked sick and frail, every bit of his sixtysomething years, and more. The hale, red-faced giant she'd grown up with had suddenly become a weak old man. It was a startling transformation.

"Senator."

Faye pinned her daughter to the doorway with her steely eyes. "Sharyn, I think you've done enough!"

Caison looked at Sharyn. His startling blue eyes were at odds with the oxygen tube in his nose and the IV line in his arm. "Come in, Sharyn."

"Caison," Faye protested. "Don't make yourself sick."

He smiled at her and kissed her hand. "Faye, leave me alone with her, please."

"What are you doing?" she demanded.

"I need to talk to Sharyn alone. I know you don't like hospitals. Why don't you go with Selma and get some lunch? Go home and change clothes. Put on something pretty for me."

"Caison, I won't be set aside this way! Sharyn was partially responsible for what happened to you." She looked at her daughter. "I'm afraid to leave you alone with her."

"Come on, Faye," Ernie coaxed. "This is your daughter you're talking about! She's no more responsible for what happened to the senator than you are. He's made his decisions, let her try to help him."

Sloane stood by the senator's bedside. "Do you want me to leave as well, sir?"

"Yes, Sloane. What I have to say is something that's better said one-on-one. The sheriff and I have some things we have to discuss."

"Yes, sir. Call if you need me. I'll be in the hall."

Sharyn settled into a chair by the window as she waited for everyone to leave the room. Sloane closed the door behind him. The security guards started to protest, but Sharyn waved them back.

"You know, I took your father up to the Diamond Back trail for the first time. He was thirteen, just turned. I was a camp counselor. He and I stayed friends, despite our difference in ages. I was there the day that you were born. T. Raymond was a strong man, but he cried that day. He loved you more than any man I've ever known could love a child."

"I know the two of you were close."

"He was a good man. A better man than he should have been." He looked down at his heavily veined hands on the white sheets. "He was a better man than I."

Sharyn sat silently, waiting for him to come to the point.

"I wanted what he had, Sharyn. He had a loving wife. They were going to start a family. I went to a convention in Las Vegas. A lawyer's convention. I met Edie the first night and I felt like lightning struck me. She was so beautiful. We talked all night long, then watched the sunrise together."

"Then you married her?"

"I did," he admitted with a sigh. "I wanted a wife who loved me and children who ran to meet me at the door. For a few days, I thought it could be Edie."

"What happened?"

He shrugged. "I had plans for my life. I wanted to be someone. I was *expected* to be someone. I was a *Talbot!* I woke up the third day and realized that I couldn't take an uneducated showgirl home and present her to my parents. It had been wonderful being with her, but it wouldn't have worked out in the real world. So I left her there, sleeping. I took what I had out of my wallet and left it for her. Then I came home to Diamond Springs."

"And you never heard from her again?"

"Actually, I did," he confessed. "A few years later, she called me out of the blue. She needed some money. She said she was desperate. I was afraid if I sent her anything that I'd never hear the end of it. She knew I came from a well-to-do family. I'd been stupid enough to tell her that much. I'd been granted an annulment, but that wouldn't stop her from calling and asking for money whenever she felt like it."

"So you told her no."

He nodded pitifully. "I did. I told her if she asked me for money again that I would find a way to make her life miserable. I told her that I wasn't married, and anything she said wouldn't matter. I was still going to have my career and she wasn't going to stop me."

"That was harsh."

"The only other person who knew was my father. He helped me get the annulment. He told me what to say to her. He swore she was going to try to blackmail me, that she'd ruin my life. I believed him."

Sharyn took a deep breath. "Senator, did you know Edith was here in Diamond Springs?"

"I had no idea. Not until I read her name in the obituary section of the *Gazette*. Even then I thought it wasn't her. I hadn't spoken to her in a lifetime. Why would she have come here to die?"

"We don't know that, sir. But I need to ask you a few questions, and you're going to have to be totally honest with me if you want me to help you."

He turned his head. "There's nothing you can do for me."

"Because the D.A. has you targeted?"

"Why would you want to help? You and I have never seen eye to eye!"

"That has nothing to do with you being innocent of this crime," she replied sincerely. "I can help you. *If* you'll tell me what's going on."

Caison looked back at her with a strange light in

his eyes. "You know, I dated your Aunt Selma once or twice. You're a lot like her. She's a strong woman who knows her mind."

"And that's why nothing ever came of it?"

He laughed, wheezing a little. "Exactly! Can you imagine me being married to a strong-minded woman? We'd kill one another!"

She smiled.

"Ask me your questions, Sheriff. I have nothing to lose at this point."

"Did you go to see Edith while she was here?"

"No! I told you, I wasn't even sure it *was* the same person when I read the obituary in the paper. I had no idea she was here."

"Would you have gone to see her if you'd known?"

He looked around the room. "I don't know. It's been thirty years. Maybe. If I'd known that she was ill."

"Why were you at the mill the day you were shot?"

"I was supposed to be there, if you recall. I just went early to have some time to think about things."

Sharyn shrugged. "But you didn't see who shot you? You didn't see or talk to Willy Newsome?"

"No. I never met that man. I didn't see who shot me."

"If you're sticking to that story, I can't help you."

"He's got me then, hasn't he?"

"You mean Jack Winter?"

"You know who I mean!" He looked out the window. "I should have killed him while I had the chance!"

"Nick has already finished the preliminary autopsy on Marcy, Senator." Caison grimaced. "Do we have to talk about this?"

"How did she die?"

"I didn't kill her."

"That's not what I asked you."

"She committed suicide. Jack knows that. She'd been at a hospital in Boulder for depression. She'd tried before. They did everything they could for her. But she stole the orderlies' keys one night and overdosed on sleeping pills. She was dead before they got to her. They called me an hour later. That's one he can't get me with—there are hospital records to back me up."

"Why wasn't it ever reported?"

"I was a senator already. I didn't want anyone to know, for my career as well as Marcy's memory. She was a high-strung woman. She couldn't handle the daily stress of political life. I didn't realize in time to save her."

"What's the name of the hospital?" Sharyn asked him, taking out her notebook.

"Stowe. It's a private hospital in Boulder. Her doctor was Dr. Chesney. You can check, if you're so inclined."

Sharyn wrote down the names. "Senator, you have to tell me why you were at the old mill early Sunday morning."

"The two aren't involved."

"They are in my mind. The D.A. is going to make the case that you knew that Edith was in town. You went to her and smothered her with a pillow so she couldn't tell anyone the things she knew about you, embarrassing you. Maybe even make you lose the election this year. Willy Newsome recognized you when you came out of the motel room. He went in, stole the things he found, then tried to blackmail you at the mill that morning. You refused. He took a pot-shot at you to let you know he was serious. Maybe you even threatened him. Winter freed him and you went after him with your gun to make sure he didn't try again."

"That's preposterous!"

"Is it? The two bullets in Willy's body came from *your* .45 Firestorm, that the D.A. just happened to find in a trash can a few blocks away from where Willy's body was found."

"I haven't used that gun since I first got it! I fired it a few times then put it away."

"How many people on a jury do you think you can convince of that?"

"I don't know! I—"

"Why were you at the mill that morning, Senator?"

"Sharyn, I—"

"I think that's enough for now, Sheriff," the senator's doctor interrupted as he returned to the room. "I asked you not to upset him. I think you should leave."

Sharyn opened her mouth to protest. She felt that she was so near the truth; she might never come that near again.

"Sheriff!" The doctor demanded her attention. "He's not your prisoner yet! He's still my patient!"

"I'm leaving," she said. She handed the senator a card with her cell phone number on it. "Call me. Anytime. I can't help you if you won't let me."

Sharyn's cell phone rang as soon a she switched it back on. "Sheriff Howard."

"I need you to come to my office," Nick told her. "There's something you should see."

"I'm upstairs. I'll be right down."

"Well?" Ernie said when she emerged into the waiting area.

"He says he didn't kill Edith or Willy. He did finally admit that he and Edith were married."

I guess that was something." He watched her press the basement button on the elevator. "Somethin' up?"

"Nick says he has something."

"I hope it's something big. That's the only thing that's gonna keep the senator out of jail at this point."

"Are you finally on my side?"

Ernie's face crinkled into a grin. "I'm always on your side, Sheriff. Hadn't you noticed that?"

The elevator doors parted and Keith met them. "Come on! Wait until you see!"

"You know, there's something not right about being that excited about dead people," Ernie told her as they followed the boy.

"I take exception to that," Nick remarked. "But this isn't about a dead person anyway. It's about DNA."

"Okay." Ernie shrugged. "What's up?"

"I was telling Sharyn earlier about a strand of hair I found closed in the photo album. It didn't match Edith's hair, though the brown pigment is the same. I borrowed a strand from the senator. It wasn't his. With all of the other stuff on that book, I wasn't sure if it mattered. I tried to match it to Willy. Still nothing."

"Nick—"

"Look!" he instructed Sharyn and Ernie.

Sharyn looked at the report he gave her. "It looks the same."

"This strand came from the musket that was fired in the old mill. The only musket that was fired, according to my friend. He finally got back with me today."

"What the name on the musket?" Ernie asked.

"Shawn Devereaux."

"Let's get something out on him."

"Have you found it anywhere else?" Sharyn recalled their earlier conversation.

"No. I probably wouldn't have found it on the musket, but it has a unique firing mechanism that it got trapped in."

"I guess it would be hard to make sure you never lost a hair while you were committing a crime," Ernie quipped.

"More importantly, this third strand is one I found stuck in Edith Randolph's birthstone ring."

"I thought you said she didn't fight her attacker?"

Nick shook his head. "I don't have an explanation for it yet. But the DNA shows a match. These strands came from people who are related to each other."

Sharyn studied the three strands of hair. "Related? Maybe she touched him before he smothered her."

"It would have to be something like that, since it didn't appear to be laying on her randomly like he'd lost it."

"So this musket belongs to Shawn Devereaux?" Ernie focused on what made sense to him. "Does he have some kind of background?"

"I couldn't find anything on him," Nick said. "I think you'll just have to pick him up."

"Where's he from?"

"Harmony," Nick answered. "Edith Randolph's son has been here the whole time."

SHARYN DROPPED ERNIE off at the office and went back to the hospital. Whether the doctor liked it or not, she was going to have to see the senator again. The story wasn't finished. She met Sloane coming out of the senator's hospital room. He closed the door behind him as he saw her.

"The senator's been sedated," his aide told her. "He was in quite a state after you left. I've never seen him this way. It's frightening."

"Did he say anything to you?"

"Only that he was sorry for everything. He didn't say exactly what. He's a beaten man, Sheriff. People he thought he could trust have betrayed him. It might have been better if he *had* died in the D.A.'s office."

"Surely not, Mr. Phillips!"

Sloane shook his head. His look was one of total dejection.

"I'll come back," Sharyn promised. "Give me a call if he wakes up before I can get here?"

"Of course, Sheriff," he agreed. "If anyone can help him, I think you can."

"Thanks. I'll probably regret it later, but I'm going to do my best."

DISTRICT ATTORNEY Jack Winter filed two counts of murder along with one count of attempted assault with a deadly weapon against Senator Caison Talbot in criminal court that afternoon. He was glad to take reporters' questions, admitting he'd been wrong about the senator's last wife, and that they'd confirmed that Marcy had been undergoing psychiatric treatment at the time of her death. The senator had covered it up, but he wasn't responsible for what had happened to her.

"Funny how he claims he's not responsible, but you just get the feeling that he means the opposite," Ed mentioned as they watched Jack Winter in action on television.

"He's got the devil's silver tongue," Trudy told him, picking up her raincoat and hat. "He can make people believe what he wants them to believe."

The storm was closing in around them, making the evening preternaturally dark. It began to rain lightly, no hint of the hail and damaging winds that were supposed to be headed towards them yet.

"Good night, Trudy," Sharyn said as the other woman was leaving.

"Good night, Sheriff. Don't stay too late."

Sharyn poured herself a fresh cup of coffee and watched the television thoughtfully. Ed was leaving with Cari. They called out their goodbyes. Ernie was out with Joe, picking up Shawn Devereaux from his construction job in Charlotte.

The thunder started to roll down from the mountains, rattling the windows and shaking the air.

Flashes of lightning blazed through the dark sky outside the office window.

Her cell phone rang and she jumped, answering quickly. "Sheriff Howard."

"Sharyn?" The senator's voice was weak but distinct on the other end.

"Yes, sir?"

"I wanted you to know. I was at the mill that morning to meet my son. He—"

The phone went dead in her hands.

TEN

"SENATOR?"

It was probably just a lightning strike at one of the cell phone towers, but she still felt uneasy. Maybe it was just the storm. Maybe it was staring at Jack Winter's face as he delivered his best friend to the criminal court system.

Whatever it was, Sharyn decided it was time to go back and talk to the senator again. This time, the doctor would have to put his concerns on hold.

Something was tickling her fingers as she held her car keys. She looked down and saw a raven-black hair entwined in the ring that held her keys. She didn't need DNA to tell her whose it was and how it got there. She recalled putting her fingers through Nick's hair when they'd been together in the Jeep. A pleasurable smile crept over her face and her cheeks got hot.

"Enough *mooning*," she told herself harshly. "Let's go!"

She put on her poncho and stood at the door into the parking lot, facing the black night and the raging storm. Before she could think about it anymore, she ran out into the storm. Her boots squelched in the wet gravel and dirt. Lightning flashed and the lights in the parking lot went dim. She reached her Jeep as the rain started coming down harder and quickly climbed inside.

Her cell phone was still dead. She tried the radio but it was worse. The streets were empty as she drove down to the hospital. The windshield wipers could barely keep pace with the heavy rain and debris flying through the air. Getting to the hospital took more time than if she'd walked it in better weather. She parked under the protective canopy and shook out her poncho before she entered the building.

Sharyn considered the senator's last words to her. He *did* know that he had a son. How long had he known? Was that why he'd been acting so strangely?

The senator's doctor wasn't on duty, but the nurse told her that the senator had been arrested just a short while before. He was being transferred to the hospital at the county jail. They'd made the determination that it was possible to move him without endangering his health.

Sharyn wasn't surprised. The D.A. wanted to move against him as soon as possible. The nurse told her that he'd left the hospital about thirty minutes before she got there. The new county lockup was half an hour away, so he might just be arriving.

What surprised her was that the senator had use of his cell phone after being arrested. *He is a senator,* she reminded herself. He'd have some special treat-ment in jail. There were many people who thought the world of Caison Talbot. Some of them would be willing to use their influence for him.

She sat down at the nurse's desk and dialed the number of the jail. The storm grumbled around her like an old man. The night desk at the jail answered. They'd sent two guards to escort the senator in an ambulance but they hadn't heard from them yet. They assumed the storm was making the trip longer than normal.

"You're the sheriff," Restin Lewis told her. "Do something about this weather!"

"My hands are tied until after the election," she quipped. "They won't let me do that kind of stuff right now."

He laughed. "I'll let you know when they roll in, Sheriff. Take care, hear?"

"Thanks, Restin."

She put down the phone gingerly and thanked the nurse. It would take them most of the night to set the senator up at the jail. She wouldn't be able to see him again until he was processed. It looked like she could go home for the night... She wished that sounded more appealing.

On a whim and not wanting to go back to her empty house yet, Sharyn started downstairs to see if Nick had left for the night. Maybe he'd want to get a cup of coffee or something. Her cell phone rang. It was Ernie calling from Charlotte.

"This has been a waste of time. Shawn Devereaux was in Harmony, sitting up with a sick baby the morning the senator was shot. A pharmacy delivered to him at home at around the same time. He was there the day of the reenactment but no way can we link him to the murder. His mama and daddy live right next door. And he's as redheaded as you, Sheriff. None of that hair Nick has as evidence would match his. What do you want us to do?"

"Come home, Ernie. There's nothing else to do tonight. They're transporting the senator to the county lock-up. We'll have to take a look at everything again tomorrow."

"Okay. I'm going to have Joe drop me off and then he'll head home."

The storm was breaking up his voice, but she was able to understand enough to know that *who* the musket had belonged to had become irrelevant. In the back of her mind, she'd always known.

Whoever shot the senator meant to kill him. The shooter hadn't just picked up the closest weapon— he'd known which musket to use. It was deliberate. He'd been there before to familiarize himself and probably watched the reenactment.

The elevators weren't working so she took the

stairs. Her phone rang again in time for a resounding clap of thunder. "Sheriff Howard."

"Sheriff, we've got a problem on the outbound interstate ramp off of Coldwell," JP said loudly. The sound of thunder and heavy rain almost obliterated his voice.

"What's wrong, JP?"

"A tree, a *big* tree, fell on top of a car as it was driving down the ramp. David and I can't get through to the paramedics or the fire department. There's a family trapped inside the car, and a line of traffic backed up halfway to the sheriff's office!"

"I'm at the hospital," she responded. "I'll call the fire department and—" The line went dead again. She hoped that he'd heard enough to know she was on it.

She ran through the doors in the basement. The light was still on in Nick's office. "Nick! Can I use your phone?"

"Of course." He eyed her suspiciously. "Did you come all this way in a storm to use my phone?"

"There's a tree down on the outbound ramp and a family trapped in a car. These cell phones are worse than useless, and the radios aren't working," she explained, then gave instructions to the man who answered the phone at the fire department.

"Why *are* you here?" he asked when she'd hung up and dialed another emergency number.

"I came to see the senator. He called me at the office and told me that he was at the mill that morning to meet with his son."

"His son! So he *did* know about him? Is that who shot him?"

"Looks like it," she replied, after giving the word to the emergency medical team. "But it wasn't Shawn Devereaux."

"Why aren't you calling 911?"

"It's busy." She hung up the phone. "Why are you asking me so many questions?"

"I don't know. It's not every night you barge into my office, demand to use my phone, and not even say hello."

She smiled. "Hello, Nick. Goodbye, Nick. I'm going out to see if they need some help out there."

"So who *did* shoot the senator?"

"Not Willy. Not Shawn Devereaux."

"I have some good news," Nick continued. "Since the senator was here, I took the liberty of measuring his palm print."

"Nick!"

"With his permission!" He stared at her indignantly. "He isn't the one who killed Edith Randolph. His hands are bigger than the prints on the pillow."

"So we're back to square one?"

"Or worse."

Her cell phone rang again. "Sheriff Howard."

"Sheriff, we've got a problem out here in the ambulance bay. I tried calling 911 but—"

"What's wrong?" she asked the unidentified caller. "Two men are out cold here and there's an ambulance missing."

"I'll be right there."

"What now?" Nick demanded.

"There are two men unconscious in the ambulance bay and an ambulance is missing." She started for the door.

"Someone took an ambulance?"

"People go nuts in this weather. Somebody probably took it joyriding."

"What can I do?" he asked her.

"Call Ernie, Cari, Joe and Ed. Have them come into the office. I might need them the way this night is shaping up. Tell them what's happened."

"What about you?"

"I'll let you know what I find out in the ambulance bay."

"Sharyn—"

"I need you here on a decent phone line, Nick!"

"Don't try anything on your own."

"I know what I'm doing, Nick." She shook her head then ran for the stairs.

THE PARAMEDICS HAD already dispatched one unit to the accident scene. The two jail guards were on stretchers when she got there.

"What happened?" she asked the first man.

"We were bringing the senator downstairs. His aide was coming with us to the jail. He had his medication and county okayed it. I didn't see him coming at me until it was too late. Sorry, Sheriff."

She patted his shoulder. "Don't worry about it. They won't get far in this storm."

Since she was at the bottom of the building, she ran around to the front in the rain and got into her Jeep quickly. So much for canopies. The passenger door opened and Nick climbed in.

"What are you doing?" she asked, starting the engine.

"Coming with you."

"I don't have time for this, Nick! I need you to call everyone in!"

"You needed someone with a *phone* to call everyone in," he determined. "I called Ernie. He's taking care of that problem. *You* need backup. Ernie agreed. Where are you going, anyway?"

"To the old mill," she answered finally, driving away from the hospital. "That's where this whole thing started and I'm guessing that's where it will end. But you'll have to stay in the Jeep. Sloane is probably armed."

"I'm an emergency deputy. And I'm armed." He took a gun out of each pocket to show her.

"Nick." She groaned.

"He took out two armed men."

"He surprised them. They didn't know he was dangerous."

"You think he means to kill the senator?"

"I think that's what he intended from the beginning. I'm not sure why. Maybe it runs in the blood. Talbot's always been a little cold and ruthless when it comes to getting what he wants. I suppose it makes sense that his son would be, too."

The lights were out on the top of the mountain, but the lightning stretched incredible silver fingers across the old peaks. Rivulets of water ran down the street and joined streams of rain that were headed for Diamond Mountain Lake.

Sharyn put her wipers on high, along with her headlight beams. Except for the occasional flashes of lightning, the night was dark and deep around them. There was no traffic, which was a blessing. She put on her blue light but left off the siren. If she was right about them being at the mill, she might need a chance to go unnoticed before it was too late. If she was wrong, she could always join in the search when they found the ambulance out on the road.

"So you think Sloane wanted to kill Caison because Caison killed his mother at the motel?" Nick surmised, looking out at the night as they passed through town.

"I suppose that would make sense, except that

Caison's palm prints don't match the ones on the pillow that suffocated Edith Randolph."

"But Sloane doesn't know that," he reminded her.

"Six years is a long time to keep your head down," Sharyn conjectured. "I'm willing to bet that Sloane *knew* the senator was his father. If he knew that his mother had come to Diamond Springs to ruin the senator, then she was found dead…"

Nick whistled. "You mean if *Sloane* found her dead. We didn't know about her until after the attack on the senator."

"Exactly. If Sloane found her dead and assumed the senator killed her, he might have retaliated against him." She stopped the Jeep abruptly. The storm still raged around them.

Two years earlier, the tiny town of Talbot's Mill had been bypassed by a new road that didn't go through the middle of the five buildings that made up the town. It saved one of the last covered bridges in the state from being demolished, and made the town what it needed to be, a protected piece of history.

There was power in the town but it was dark that night. The general store, the museum, and the corn silo were ghostly silhouettes when the sky lit up from the dangerous lightning that was flashing around it. The old mill was a gloomy heap beside the road and the covered bridge. Water poured across the dam and dropped to the huge stones beneath, foaming and splashing uselessly. The giant waterwheel was tied up close to the building. It only harvested the water from the lake when corn was being milled.

"What about Willy?" Nick whispered into the darkness between them.

"I don't know how he figures into it yet. Maybe it was retaliation because Willy robbed his mother."

"And Sloane used the senator's gun to kill Willy to make it look worse?"

Sharyn shrugged, keeping her eyes on the old mill. "Or because he had access to it. If he'd planned on killing the senator from the beginning, he wouldn't care how it looked."

"So you're saying that Sloane hated the senator so he stayed close to him for six years? Or that he loved him and wanted to be close to him?"

"If I had all the answers, Nick, I wouldn't be sitting here with you. I'd be Miss Sharyn on the psychic buddy's network."

He laughed darkly. "Sorry. So what do we do now?"

"We see if we can find the ambulance. Then hope the senator is still alive."

They left the Jeep up on the bridge that forced the new highway around the town. Coming down like shadows inside the covered bridge, Sharyn and Nick looked around the building from the shelter of the structure. There was no sign of the ambulance on the street or alongside the mill.

Sharyn had been so sure Sloane Phillips would bring the senator here, but it appeared to be a mistake. She took out her cell phone and tried to get through to Ernie again.

Ernie answered this time. "Where are you?"

"Out at the old mill," she replied cautiously. "Once I realized—"

"What?"

"I think Sloane Phillips is the senator's son, Edith Randolph's baby."

"Sheriff, what are you talking about?"

She frowned. "Maybe nothing. The ambulance isn't out here."

"Are you out there alone?"

"No. Nick's here with me."

"I put out an APB on that ambulance, but no sign of it yet."

She answered, "I don't think they're here, either."

"Sharyn!" Nick whispered.

"Ernie, hold on."

"Look up there!" Nick pointed towards the bridge where they'd parked.

"Wait!" Sharyn said, glancing up at the underside of the new bridge. "He did what I did, Ernie. Except he parked *under* the new bridge. That's why we couldn't see him!"

There was no response but static. Sharyn put the phone back into her pocket. She knew Ernie well enough that if he didn't hear from her again, he would come out to see what was going on. She looked up at the old mill and saw a light flicker feebly through one of the tiny windows. She knew she couldn't wait. It might already be too late.

"What now?" Nick asked, following the line of her vision.

"We can't just shoot our way in there. We know Sloane is motivated to kill the senator. They could both wind up dead."

"We need a distraction," he agreed.

Sharyn nodded. "Take my poncho. Go up and knock on the door. We used to climb along the ledge to that window up there when I was a kid. I can sneak in that way if we can get him to answer the door."

"Why the poncho?" he wondered, taking it from her.

She grinned. "Who is going to see you in a suit coat and believe you work at the mill?"

"So, I'm the miller?"

"You got it."

"Weapons?"

"Let's assume that he's armed and he might have killed at least once. Keep your gun under the poncho, Nick. And be careful. Don't take any chances. Tell him you saw the light and were afraid something was wrong. Don't try to arrest him! If he comes down, let him talk, then go away. That should be enough time for me."

"I've been out in the field before," he reminded her drily.

"I know. But this is a *live* body, Nick! Give me five minutes, then go up to the door."

"Don't worry about me! I'm not the one who has to show everyone else up. I heard about the motel thing, you know!"

She ignored him. "Try to call Ernie again while you're waiting. Let him know what we're doing."

He nodded, glancing up at the light in the window three stories up. He started to caution her but she was already gone.

Drawing her gun, Sharyn carefully stayed in the shadows along the street to the mill. She was soaked, but the thunder would mask any noise she would make getting there. She hoped that Sloane hadn't realized yet that his plan hadn't worked out.

She ran up the outdoor stairs to a ledge that was used to unblock the wheel when debris came over the dam. The concrete was rough, so she wasn't worried about sliding even though the rain was washing over the edge. She'd neglected to tell Nick that there was only one way to reach that window. She would have to crawl up the side of the tethered waterwheel.

Sharyn looked down at the water rushing over the

dam. She took a deep breath and forced herself not to look down again. She put one foot into a bucket and then grabbed another one. Hand-over-hand, she climbed from one bucket to the next. The waterwheel trembled with her movements. She wondered about the strength of the tether that held it, but there was no other way into the building. It was strange to think that as a child, she'd longed to climb up the big wheel. On closer inspection, she could have lived without the experience. As she got nearer to the window, she could hear voices from the building.

"What did you think would happen to us, old man?" Sloane was demanding from Caison. "My mother was alone and penniless when she called you for help. You turned her down!"

"I didn't know about you," Caison answered in a plaintive voice Sharyn didn't recognize. "I swear, Edie didn't tell me she was pregnant."

"What difference does it make? Would you have helped her if you'd known about me?"

"I—I don't know. We were only together three days, Sloane! How could I have known?"

"You killed her!" Sloane raged. "I thought I could get close to you. I thought you'd think of me as a son. I thought someday I could tell you who I was and we could have some kind of family."

"We could still be a family," Caison pleaded. "I regret your mother's passing, son, but—"

"Passing?" The younger man's voice was choked. "Why couldn't *you* have died sooner?"

"Sloane, I hardly think that's fair!"

"Fair? Was it *fair* what you did to her? Was it *fair* how you ruined her life? Was it *fair* what you made me do?"

"Look, son," Caison continued, his voice trembling, "I know you want to hurt me, but I understand your anger. We can put this behind us."

Sloane's laugh was a terrible, rasping sound. "How do *we* put this behind us, *Dad?* You killed her slowly for years. But I finished it."

"What are you saying?" Caison asked, shocked.

"What do you think I'm saying, old man?"

Caison was silent. Sharyn heard what she thought must be Sloane's booted feet pacing the old wooden floor.

"She came here to die. She wanted you to take the blame for it. She *hated* you! I offered to kill you a dozen times. I thought if you were dead, she'd just let go and it wouldn't matter. But you wouldn't die! I had no choice."

"Are you saying you killed your mother? You killed Edie?"

Sharyn had reached the top of the waterwheel. She laid flat on it, catching her breath. She could see inside the window, glad for the candle inside and the darkness outside. She hoped they wouldn't see her. The catch on the window was loose.

Sloane reached back and slapped the senator. The sound echoed in the empty mill. "*You* killed her! I might have put the pillow over her face but *you killed her!*"

"Sloane, you don't know what you're saying! Let me get you a lawyer. Or better yet, let's leave the country together. I know people who would be willing to help us. You wouldn't have to face this—" The senator's head snapped back with the next blow.

Sharyn heard the knock on the door echo through the mill. She closed her eyes, wishing she could wipe the water from her face but not daring to let go of the wheel. *Answer the door!*

Sloane put his hands across the senator's mouth and waited for the knocking to subside. He crouched down beside the older man and remained motionless. The knocking faded.

So much for that plan!

"Do you think I'd go anywhere with you?" Sloane began ranting again, but in a hushed tone. "You and I are going to finish what I started here that morning."

"You can't kill me!" Talbot sounded more like himself.

"I should've killed you that night! But maybe Mom was right. Maybe this is better. They're going to blame you for everything. You'll be too guilty to live, so you take your own life."

Caison laughed. "No one will ever believe that I killed myself!"

"They believe that you murdered two people, Senator! How much of a stretch will it be, that you couldn't live with yourself?"

Caison was sitting on the stone floor, leaning against the back wall of the building. The candle-light flickered on his drawn face. "I'm your own flesh and blood, son! You're a *Talbot!*"

"Maybe that means something to you, but to me it only means that you let us live poor and alone while you had everything you wanted. My mother had noth-ing to give me, except her hatred for you! I did what she wanted me to do but I'm not willing to take a chance that you might get off." Sloane took out the second gun registered in the senator's name.

"Sloane, you must feel something for me. You've stayed with me, knowing I was your father. I didn't know you were my son but I've treated you like my own. Please, consider my offer. We could leave now and never look back."

"Mom and I had everything set up so perfectly for the police to find. They should have known immedi-ately who she was and why you'd killed her. Instead, they took her in as Jane Doe because that animal stole her dignity and ruined everything. I didn't mind killing him for that. Do you think I mind killing you for everything you did to her?"

Sloane put the gun to the senator's head, and Sharyn knew she couldn't wait any longer. She kicked in the window, splintering the old frame. Rain poured in from the storm as it beat on the old mill. "Get away from him, Sloane."

"Sheriff!"

Sloane held the gun steadily on the senator. "I've come this far— Do you think I care if I'm caught or if you kill me?"

His hand on the gun was shaking. His voice trembled. Sharyn knew he was almost beyond reason. "Put down the gun, Sloane. Let's talk."

"I've said what I have to say, Sheriff. There's just this one thing left to do. After that, I don't care what you do."

"This isn't the way to hurt him. Don't you know him well enough by now to know that?"

Sloane looked at her. He was crying. "Do you have any idea how many things I've seen him squirm out of? This is the one thing I won't let him gloss over!"

"If you kill him, no one will ever know the truth about your mother," Sharyn reasoned, taking a step closer to him.

"Wh-what are you saying?"

"They'll think you killed her, then killed him out of spite. He'll get away with what he did to the two of you. The only way you can tell your story and make people listen is for both of you to stay alive."

While he thought over her words, Sharyn kept her eye on him. His hand slipped a little, the gun moving away from Talbot's head. She didn't wait. Grabbing the gun, she twisted it from his hand. She leaned close to push him away from the senator when Caison threw cornmeal in her face, blinding her.

"Run!" he yelled at Sloane. "You still have time! Go quickly!"

Sharyn inhaled the cornmeal and choked on it. She wiped it from her nose and mouth.

"Not until you're dead," Sloane declared and shoved the senator towards Sharyn.

Sharyn heard the wooden frame splinter around her as she and the senator both fell through it. She had the feeling of weightlessness while it seemed that she was suspended in midair. Then there was the awful plunge.

She knew she couldn't protect herself from the rocks in the water below the dam. The senator was pressed against her as they fell together. She couldn't turn to dive and try to avoid the sharp points. She didn't know if it would do any good in the blackness anyway. She closed her eyes and tried to believe what Marvella had said about her father's spirit protecting her. It was all she had left.

The water closed around her, warm and black.

Sharyn said a prayer of thanks and kicked free from the senator. She surfaced for air. The water splashed down from the dam and thundered in her ears. She caught sight of the senator's white face just before he sank beneath the water. Taking a deep breath, she swam after him, finally catching him under the arms and towing him towards the edge of the water. Breathing hard, she put her head to his chest. He was unconscious but still breathing.

"Need a hand?" Ernie asked as a bright light shone down on them from the covered bridge. "Or are you gonna do it all yourself?"

PARAMEDICS BROUGHT THE ambulance down the hill for the senator. He had suffered another mild heart attack. They transported him to the hospital in Diamond Springs again.

Caison glared at Sharyn as they took him past her. "I won't testify against him! Everything he said to me is privileged. You can't use any of it!"

Sharyn sat beside the mill on an old grist stone under a tin overhang. Ed had wrapped a blanket around her shoulders and given her a hug with it. She looked away from Caison, for the first time feeling more pity than scorn for the old man. He had paid a terrible price for his arrogance and his mistakes.

"You okay?" Ernie asked her, flicking some wet cornmeal out of her hair.

"Yeah. I'm just glad it was only cornmeal. Two mistakes in less than a week. Either one could have killed me."

"You'll learn," he assured her with a patronizing voice. "It takes time, but everyone does."

"Thanks." She glanced around at all the activity going on in the mill. "Where's Nick?"

"He made his first arrest. That Phillips boy came running out of the mill and Nick was on him like a hog at the trough! We were just pulling up. I trained him, you know. I'm proud of the boy! But he has to do his paperwork. So, what made you come out here?"

She explained what she knew and what she'd heard in the mill.

"You believe Edith set it up for him to kill her before she died to make it look like the senator did it?"

"Sloane said they were desperately poor, and at one point Edith had called and asked the senator for money. I guess she didn't tell him that he had a son. He said no. She taught Sloane to hate him, too."

Ernie shook his head sadly. "It might have made a difference if she'd told him. That man has always wanted a child. Marcy couldn't have children. Now his own son has tried to kill him."

"It reminds me of my question to you about your friends becoming homeless after being heroes. I guess there aren't any answers for some things."

"I can't wait to read your report," he confessed.

"You're going to have to wait, because I'm going home. I'm going to wash this cornmeal off and go to bed!"

"Good. I'll drive you. That way I won't have to wait for the report."

EPILOGUE

AT ERNIE'S REQUEST, they gathered at the veteran's cemetery outside of town. Seven soldiers stepped forward after the plain casket was in place over the grave. Staff Sergeant Eldeon Percy shouted his commands, and the guns raised and fired three times. The sound echoed back from the mountains.

Ernie stood at attention in his uniform alongside Fred Sandler, who'd outgrown his old uniform and had to wear a dark suit. Monty stood beside him in a new dark suit that Ernie had purchased for him. Joe stood in military dress uniform next to him.

Sheriff Sharyn Howard, in standard sheriff's dress uniform, stood beside Ed behind the other men. They saluted as the last shot was fired and the bugle was sounding taps. Ernie accepted the exquisitely folded American flag, and Captain Willy Newsome's purple heart from the sergeant. The casket was lowered into the warm, Carolina soil.

"So, SLOANE PLED GUILTY?" Nick asked as he picked up another handful of popcorn.

"Yep," Sharyn said, sitting beside him on the floor

in front of the television in his apartment, watching the news. "I think he took to heart what I said about everyone knowing what the senator did to him. He really wanted to tell his story."

"He had this revelation *after* he threw you out of the window, right?"

"Better late than never, I suppose."

"What about the senator?"

"He's out of the hospital, recovering at home. My mother won't take his calls. The press is calling for his resignation. The senate is launching an investigation into his affairs. He'll be prosecuted for a minor assault charge unless Michaelson still has some pull with the D.A."

"How many affairs did he have?" Nick queried, eating another handful of popcorn.

"Next time, you supply the popcorn," she reprimanded. "This big bowl would have lasted me for a week! And I don't mean romantic affairs, I mean—"

"I know what you mean. And *I* made this popcorn."

"I feel sorry for him, Nick. I can't believe it, but I do. And I *brought* the popcorn!"

A breaking news story flashed across the screen. Nick sighed. "Now what?"

"The District Attorney for Diamond Springs has just announced his candidacy for senator from that district."

Jack Winter's face appeared on the screen. "In light of everything that's happened, I feel we cannot allow Caison Talbot to represent our district again in the senate. Since he has been running unopposed, I have agreed to step in and run against him for senator."

Nick shook his head. "Give the devil his due."

* * * * *

REQUEST YOUR FREE BOOKS!
2 FREE NOVELS PLUS 2 FREE GIFTS!

HARLEQUIN

INTRIGUE

BREATHTAKING ROMANTIC SUSPENSE

YES! Please send me 2 FREE Harlequin Intrigue® novels and my 2 FREE gifts (gifts are worth about $10). After receiving them, if I don't wish to receive any more books, I can return the shipping statement marked "cancel." If I don't cancel, I will receive 6 brand-new novels every month and be billed just $4.74 per book in the U.S. or $5.24 per book in Canada. That's a savings of at least 14% off the cover price! It's quite a bargain! Shipping and handling is just 50¢ per book in the U.S. and 75¢ per book in Canada.* I understand that accepting the 2 free books and gifts places me under no obligation to buy anything. I can always return a shipment and cancel at any time. Even if I never buy another book, the two free books and gifts are mine to keep forever.

182/382 HDN F43C

Name _____ (PLEASE PRINT)

Address _____ Apt. #

City _____ State/Prov. _____ Zip/Postal Code

Signature (if under 18, a parent or guardian must sign)

Mail to the **Harlequin® Reader Service:**
IN U.S.A.: P.O. Box 1867, Buffalo, NY 14240-1867
IN CANADA: P.O. Box 609, Fort Erie, Ontario L2A 5X3

**Are you a subscriber to Harlequin Intrigue books
and want to receive the larger-print edition?
Call 1-800-873-8635 or visit www.ReaderService.com.**

* Terms and prices subject to change without notice. Prices do not include applicable taxes. Sales tax applicable in N.Y. Canadian residents will be charged applicable taxes. Offer not valid in Quebec. This offer is limited to one order per household. Not valid for current subscribers to Harlequin Intrigue books. All orders subject to credit approval. Credit or debit balances in a customer's account(s) may be offset by any other outstanding balance owed by or to the customer. Please allow 4 to 6 weeks for delivery. Offer available while quantities last.

Your Privacy—The Harlequin® Reader Service is committed to protecting your privacy. Our Privacy Policy is available online at www.ReaderService.com or upon request from the Harlequin Reader Service.

We make a portion of our mailing list available to reputable third parties that offer products we believe may interest you. If you prefer that we not exchange your name with third parties, or if you wish to clarify or modify your communication preferences, please visit us at www.ReaderService.com/consumerschoice or write to us at Harlequin Reader Service Preference Service, P.O. Box 9062, Buffalo, NY 14269. Include your complete name and address.

HIDIR13R

REQUEST YOUR
FREE BOOKS!

2 FREE NOVELS
FROM THE SUSPENSE COLLECTION
PLUS 2 FREE GIFTS!

YES! Please send me 2 FREE novels from the Suspense Collection and my 2 FREE gifts (gifts are worth about $10). After receiving them, if I don't wish to receive any more books, I can return the shipping statement marked "cancel." If I don't cancel, I will receive 4 brand-new novels every month and be billed just $6.24 per book in the U.S. or $6.74 per book in Canada. That's a savings of at least 22% off the cover price. It's quite a bargain! Shipping and handling is just 50¢ per book in the U.S. and 75¢ per book in Canada.* I understand that accepting the 2 free books and gifts places me under no obligation to buy anything. I can always return a shipment and cancel at any time. Even if I never buy another book, the two free books and gifts are mine to keep forever.

191/391 MDN F4XN

Name _____ (PLEASE PRINT)

Address _____ Apt. #

City _____ State/Prov. _____ Zip/Postal Code

Signature (if under 18, a parent or guardian must sign)

Mail to the Harlequin® Reader Service:
IN U.S.A.: P.O. Box 1867, Buffalo, NY 14240-1867
IN CANADA: P.O. Box 609, Fort Erie, Ontario L2A 5X3

Want to try two free books from another line?
Call 1-800-873-8635 or visit www.ReaderService.com.

* Terms and prices subject to change without notice. Prices do not include applicable taxes. Sales tax applicable in N.Y. Canadian residents will be charged applicable taxes. Offer not valid in Quebec. This offer is limited to one order per household. Not valid for current subscribers to the Suspense Collection or the Romance/Suspense Collection. All orders subject to credit approval. Credit or debit balances in a customer's account(s) may be offset by any other outstanding balance owed by or to the customer. Please allow 4 to 6 weeks for delivery. Offer available while quantities last.

Your Privacy—The Harlequin® Reader Service is committed to protecting your privacy. Our Privacy Policy is available online at www.ReaderService.com or upon request from the Harlequin Reader Service.

We make a portion of our mailing list available to reputable third parties that offer products we believe may interest you. If you prefer that we not exchange your name with third parties, or if you wish to clarify or modify your communication preferences, please visit us at www.ReaderService.com/consumerschoice or write to us at Harlequin Reader Service Preference Service, P.O. Box 9062, Buffalo, NY 14269. Include your complete name and address.

ReaderService.com

Manage your account online!

- Review your order history
- Manage your payments
- Update your address

*We've designed
the Harlequin® Reader Service
website just for you.*

Enjoy all the features!

- Reader excerpts from any series
- Respond to mailings and
  special monthly offers
- Discover new series available to you
- Browse the Bonus Bucks catalog
- Share your feedback

Visit us at:
ReaderService.com